Praise for

1 *New York Times* bestselling author
STEPHANIE LAURENS

"Her lush sensuality takes my breath away!"
New York Times bestselling author
Lisa Kleypas

~

New York Times bestselling author
GAELEN FOLEY

"Foley's wonderful romance will appeal to
Amanda Quick and Stephanie Laurens fans."
Booklist

~

New York Times bestselling author
LORETTA CHASE

"One of the finest romance authors of all time."
New York Times bestselling author
Julia Quinn

By Stephanie Laurens

The Lady Risks All

The Black Cobra Quartet
The Untamed Bride
The Elusive Bride
The Brazen Bride
The Reckless Bride

Bastion Club Novels
Captain Jack's Woman (prequel)
The Lady Chosen
A Gentleman's Honor
A Lady of His Own
A Fine Passion
To Distraction
Beyond Seduction
The Edge of Desire
Mastered By Love

The Cynster Novels
Devil's Bride
A Rake's Vow
Scandal's Bride

ROYAL BRIDESMAIDS

Stephanie
LAURENS

Gaelen
FOLEY

Loretta
CHASE

AVON

An Imprint of HarperCollinsPublishers

CONTENTS

A Return Engagement

STEPHANIE LAURENS

"*There* she is!" Hereditary Prince Frederick of Lautenberg, heir apparent to the principality, beamed as he watched his princess-to-be emerge onto the deck of the royal barge as it angled to approach the dock.

Standing beside Frederick, Robert Knightley, second son of the Earl of Rockingham, smiled as Frances Daughtry, a sweet, slender, fair-haired English rose, raised a hesitant hand in response to the crowd's cheers. Frances would, in Robert's estimation, be the perfect Princess. Aside from her excellent pedigree and the inbred manners that went with that, her refined and elegant beauty, and her experience in the socially demanding arena of the ton, she was English, and as the British envoy to the Court of Lautenberg as well as the Prince's closest friend, confidant, and personal advisor, Robert definitely approved of that.

Installing Frances, the youngest daughter of the Duke of Pemberton, as the Hereditary Princess of Lautenberg was a coup with which the British government and Robert's masters in the Foreign Office were openly thrilled. And while Robert hadn't played Cupid—Frederick had met Frances in London during a short visit the previous year and had been instantly smitten—he nevertheless felt that in facilitating the budding romance and steering it to a successful conclusion he'd discharged his duties on all fronts in exemplary fashion.

Frances turned her head, apparently listening to someone behind her, then faced forward, walked to the railing, and smiled and waved more definitely.

Delighted, the crowd roared, waved, and cheered back. Huzzahs filled the air; a faint breeze whisked over the water, making the flags strung up all around snap and flutter. Frederick, Robert noted, could not have been more pleased. Good. Everything was progressing smoothly.

Returning his gaze to the deck of the barge, sent to ferry the princess-to-be from the mouth of the Rhine, he surveyed the others in the bridal party as they emerged on deck. They'd traveled from London by ship to the Rhine mouth, then transferred to the barge for the trip upriver to Koblenz, before turning southward on the Mosel. The Mosel formed the eastern border of Lautenberg, and the principality's capital, Kremunz, stood on its western shore.

Robert recognized the tall figure of the Duke of Pemberton, with his duchess, Valeria, in her signature gauzy draperies, on his arm. Beside them, directly behind Frances's right shoulder, stood . . .

The person to whom Frances had listened. Robert blinked and looked again, but the tall, willowy, dark-haired lady, a few inches taller than Frances, did not transmogrify into either of her shorter, fair-haired sisters. "What the devil . . . ?"

Frederick—beneath his delighted veneer the prospective groom was distinctly nervous—cast him a sharp glance. "What is it?"

Schooling his features, Robert shook his head dismissively. "Just someone in the party I hadn't realized would be coming." Someone he certainly hadn't expected.

Someone he hadn't expected to see, not up close, not to speak with, much less to organize

and oversee a wedding with . . . As he scanned
the remainder of the bridal party, that last became
all too clear. Frances's other two sisters, Felicity
and Esme, weren't there. For some godforsaken
reason, Lady Cornelia Daughtry had stepped into
the shoes he'd been told her other sisters would
fill.

"*S*ee?" Lady Cornelia Daughtry, Nell to those
close to her, murmured soothingly, reassuringly,
just loudly enough for her sister to hear. "I told
you they'd be delighted. Just listen to those cheers.
And as for your Frederick, if he smiles any more
widely his face will crack . . ."

Nell's gaze had traveled beyond Frederick; her
eyes widened, her lungs seized.

At her sudden silence, Frances, still facing the
cheering hordes, nervously murmured, "What
is it?"

Thanking the stars Frances couldn't turn
around and see her face, Nell continued to stare at
the man standing beside Prince Frederick. "Nothing. Just keep smiling and waving and looking
delighted. That's all you need to do."

Finally dragging in a decent breath, Nell looked
sideways and caught their mother's eye. Lowering

her voice even further, she whispered, "Were you expecting Robert Knightley to be here?"

Valeria, Duchess of Pemberton, blinked her large violet eyes. "Why, yes, dear, of course. Robert is Prince Frederick's closest friend and diplomatic right arm, as it were." Looking past Frances to where Robert stood on the docks with Frederick and the rest of the official welcoming party, Valeria smiled. "As the British envoy to Lautenberg, dear Robert is in charge of all the arrangements. Should we require any assistance, it is to him we should appeal."

With a wordless "ah," Nell turned back to the prospect before her. One she hadn't until that moment realized lay before her.

A long-ago would-be husband who, while he'd never actually come up to the mark, had effectively spoiled her for all others.

That was how she saw Robert Knightley.

He looked well. She could admit that. Could let her gaze sweep over his broad shoulders, down the long length of his leanly muscled frame, before returning to the chiseled, patrician planes of his face with some small degree of detachment.

At least while several feet of river and rather more of planking separated them.

How would she manage when they were

closer? A lot closer? When she was forced to inter-
act with him on a daily, even hourly basis in the
frantic days before the wedding?

How would she fare when she and he—if he
was as close to Frederick as it seemed—perforce
walked down the aisle together?

Oh, God.

She didn't dare voice the words, and in the end
her feelings didn't matter.

She was there and so was he, and she would
simply have to manage.

*A*n hour later, standing in the castle's drawing
room with a cup of calming tea in her hand, Nell
decided the most appropriate strategy was to take
the bull by the horns.

Some angel had consented to watch over her
on the docks; in the joy and rapture of Frederick
formally greeting Frances, then welcoming their
parents, she'd managed to avoid exchanging more
than a polite nod with Robert. The entire party
had then piled into open carriages for the trip up
a long, winding, stone-paved road to the castle,
a sizeable structure in pale gray stone sporting
towers and turrets with conical roofs, crenellated
battlements, and countless pennants flying regally
in the breeze. Perched above the red roofs of the

town and the sparkling blue ribbon of the river, in the bright summer sunshine the castle possessed a fairy-tale radiance. Although Nell had been in the same carriage as Robert, indeed, although they'd sat on the same bench seat, they'd both been facing back along the cavalcade; she hadn't had to meet his eye and had taken care not to.

Their progression through the huge gates of the castle had been accompanied by a sudden drop in the surrounding noise, but almost immediately the carriages had drawn up before the steps leading into the castle keep; the extended and clearly modernized building filled much of the space within the battlemented walls. Frederick had descended first, then had handed Frances down to enthusiastic applause from the assembled courtiers. Nell had quickly followed Frances, allowing a liveried footman to assist her to the flags.

As she'd followed Frances and Frederick up the stairs and into the great hall beyond the massive double doors, she'd been intensely aware of Robert walking alongside her, but there'd been so many others to smile at and exchange polite nods with she felt sure no one had noticed that she'd kept her gaze studiously from him.

Frederick had led Frances triumphantly into a magnificent formal drawing room, and had swept her sister up to a pair of ornate thrones.

This part of the proceedings Nell and her mother had known about and had drilled Frances in thoroughly; her sister had made a very nice show of curtsying and greeting her future parents-in-law, Frederick's parents, the ageing Prince and Princess of Lautenberg. Both monarchs had been disposed to be delighted; standing behind Frances, Nell had seen her sister's tense shoulders ease.

Then Frederick had led Frances to one side, and Robert had stepped forward to introduce Nell. She had duly smiled, curtsied, risen, and had exchanged the regulation greetings and observations before stepping aside to allow her parents to come forward. She would have loved to have simply melted into the crowd, but she'd known her duty. She'd unobtrusively slipped into position behind Frances, ready to lend support when next it was needed.

But Frances had taken heart from the sincerely warm reception; as the tea service had commenced, Nell had watched her sister smile and chat with commendable spontaneity. Noting that her mother, too, was keeping a surreptitious eye on her soon-to-be-royal sibling, Nell accepted that, while she'd succeeded in avoiding Robert to that point, she couldn't avoid him for much longer.

Cup and saucer in hand, he'd retreated to stand by the wall a little way down the room. While he sipped, he constantly scanned the crowd, as any good organizer would. Balancing her own cup and saucer, she girded her loins and glided across to join him. Without meeting his eyes, she turned to stand beside him, to sip and survey the assembled courtiers, too.

He spoke first. "I had no idea you were coming."

"I had no idea you would be here."

He hesitated, then asked, "Would you have come if you'd known?"

She thought before truthfully stating, "I don't know."

From the corner of her eyes, she saw his lips twist, then he set his cup on his saucer and lightly shrugged. "It doesn't really matter, does it? Water under the bridge, so to speak."

She felt his gaze on her face, but didn't meet it, just nodded. "Indeed. My role here is to ensure that this wedding goes off without a hitch—at least from the bride's side."

He inclined his head. "And my role is the complementary one and my purpose the same, but . . . there is a wider consideration, and that not only for me, but for us both."

She frowned, glanced at him. "What wider consideration?"

Finally. Robert caught her dark violet eyes, several shades darker than her mother's, and felt the same jolt he had years ago—nine years ago to be precise. They'd seen each other over the intervening years, in passing in the ballrooms and drawing rooms of the ton, but not since they'd parted had they been this close, or looked so directly into each other's eyes.

And it was all still there—that indefinable connection, the spark of an attraction that was more than just physical, that welled from deep inside, then spread beneath their skins. Nothing had changed . . . or rather, if anything, the link had grown stronger, harder, more refined, more definite, the flash of connection more compelling.

She sensed it, too; of that he had not a single doubt. The slight hitch in her breathing, and her widening eyes, gave her away.

Those fabulous, rich pansy eyes searched his, then she blinked, and a frown started to form, drawing down her perfectly arched dark brows, setting a faint wrinkle in the unblemished expanse of her forehead; her straight nose, delicately curved lush lips, and decidedly determined feminine chin hadn't changed in the least.

What had he been saying? He denied the impulse to clear his throat. "This wedding has wider political and strategic implications for our country." He glanced briefly at the crowd in the room; no one was near enough to overhear. Although several courtiers had their eyes on Nell, eager to make her acquaintance, everyone knew he and she needed to consult about the details of the bride and groom's days, let alone the wedding, so were politely giving them some time. He returned his gaze to her. "Lautenberg is small, largely rural, and has no particular commercial significance, but strategically it's vital to our government's wider peacekeeping aims."

Her eyes on his, she nodded. "I see."

He was fairly certain she did; she was one of the most quick-witted females he'd ever encountered. "Indeed. So the government and our country have a vested interest in seeing this wedding goes off without a hitch. If you get so much as a whiff of anything not just going wrong, but not being perfectly right, let me know."

She studied him for a long moment, then inclined her head. "Very well."

He couldn't read her expression; he'd forgotten she had a particularly good, blank but alert, poker face.

Tipping her head, she continued to regard him for an instant more, then said, "I'll do that, and in return perhaps you will alert me should Frederick have any . . . concerns, or questions, of whatever sort."

He blinked.

She met his gaze for only a second more, then turned away. "As I said, do let me know."

He watched her glide into the crowd, saw several courtiers descend on her, surrounding her with smiles and offering introductions; he debated stepping in and assisting with the latter, but she was assured and experienced, and in such tame company needed no help in conquering them all.

"But what the devil did you mean, my long-ago love?" He might not be sure of much when it came to her, but from her manner, her tone, and not least her words, he was absolutely certain she knew of at least one potential source of trouble.

"*I* just don't know." Frances turned this way and that before the cheval glass, critically viewing her turquoise silk gown. "Oh, Nell—what do you think? Will I do?"

"You'll do, and that magnificently. Stop fretting. You know this panic's only to be expected, and that's why I'm here—to assure you it's all just nerves and will pass, and soon all will be well." Nell lifted a delicate necklace of aquamarines and diamonds, their parents' wedding gift to Frances, from its velvet bed. "Here—let me settle this."

She did, examining Frances's face in the mirror

while she smoothed the fine links of the necklace; thus far, her sister was holding up reasonably well. "Now don't worry—I'll be beside or just behind you while we're in the drawing room, and Mama will be nearby, too. And as Robert will have overseen the seating for the dinner, I'll be placed opposite. Although I won't be able to converse directly, I will be there should you have any problems. And I will be listening, no matter that I won't appear to be."

Stepping back, she ran her eyes once more over Frances, then nodded. "Just remember—Frederick is head over ears in love with you, no matter what that silly little voice in your head whispers."

Turning, Frances met Nell's eyes, and grinned. "Thank you, sister mine." Stretching up, Frances touched her cheek to Nell's, found Nell's fingers with hers and squeezed, then drew back.

A deep *bong* resonated throughout the palace.

"That's it—the dinner gong." Frances whirled toward the door. "We should go."

"Indeed." Moving smoothly forward, Nell paused by the door. "But without any unseemly rush."

They glided, side by side, down the long corridors and down the ornate stairs. In her dark violet-purple silk gown, a perfect foil for Frances's paler beauty, Nell drew almost as many eyes as—

and, indeed, many more openly admiring glances than—her younger sister. She was aware of the fact, but neither returned nor acknowledged any of those glances; her focus was on Frances, on being her sister's support.

The fabulously ornate drawing room—the Germanic states did so love their gilt and crystal—played host to an army of elegantly garbed courtiers, but everyone was disposed to be delighted and accommodating, and the hour Frances spent on Frederick's arm, being introduced to those who would shortly become her subjects, passed easily and without incident. Somewhat to Nell's surprise, while she'd seen Robert the instant she walked into the room—and he'd seen her—he kept his distance, leaving her able to concentrate on Frances without distraction.

For which she was grateful . . . except that not knowing where in the crush Robert actually was, knowing he was near, but not knowing in which direction, distracted her anyway.

It was almost a relief when he eventually appeared at Frederick's side to whisper in his friend's ear that dinner was about to be announced.

As a stentorian announcement that dinner was served rang out over the room, Nell steeled herself to take Robert's arm when he offered it—only to have a gentleman, one of the lords of the court, gallantly step in to offer his arm and lead her in. Uncertain of protocol and precedence in this court, she glanced at Robert; he'd been waiting to catch her glance and nodded.

Plastering on a smile, Nell inclined her head and accepted, settling her hand on the gentleman's sleeve and allowing him to lead her in her sister and Frederick's wake. Not exactly disappointed, but a trifle off-balance with the steeling of her nerves that was no longer required.

To her considerable relief, her prediction of the table placements proved to be sound; she was seated opposite Frances, with the attentive courtier beside her. At the very last, Robert took the seat on her other side, opposite Frederick, and the meal began.

One of Frederick's male cousins sat on Frances's other side, and for much of the meal, between the cousin's questions and Frederick's comments, Frances was absorbed enough to prevent any unease or uncertainty showing through. Nell, more than socially adept enough to maintain a conversation with her dinner partners while simultaneously monitoring Frances's every word, was wondering if, perhaps, the entire dinner would pass without any episode . . . when, as the dessert plates were being set out, she saw Frances press back in her chair, and start rather furtively glancing about . . .

Then Frances remembered her instructions, drew a deep breath, and looked across the table. Nell was waiting to catch her gaze, to smile and nod and, across the width of the table, project all she wished she could whisper in her sister's ear . . .

It worked. Well enough for Frances to breathe more calmly. After a moment, Frances gave a tiny nod, then Frederick spoke to her and she turned to him, and if her smile was a trifle wobbly, and significantly less strong than it had been earlier, yet still she smiled and went on.

After watching Frances for a moment more and detecting no further eruption of uncertainty, Nell inwardly sighed and shifted her attention to the courtier by her side.

From Nell's other side, Robert cast her a sharp glance, but her face was averted and he couldn't see her eyes, much less catch her gaze. But he'd seen . . . something. Whatever it was—whatever it was that had happened with Frances—it had made Nell tense. Tense as if about to spring forward to avert some incipient disaster.

Which did not bode well for a perfectly scripted wedding.

Robert glanced at her again. She was now animatedly engaged with the local lord; he could almost feel a wall between them—one she kept high.

What was it that had just happened? And what was going on?

He would, he suspected, get no chance to extract answers to those questions tonight, but answers he would have—and soon.

*R*obert did wonder if all he was detecting was caused by nothing more than the expected and excusable nerves, but Nell's continuing protectiveness, let alone her family's high social profile and the hours even the younger Frances would have spent in the most august of ton circles, all argued against that.

At the conclusion of the dinner, the entire company filed into the ballroom where the evening's soiree was to be held. The dinner guests were augmented by additional guests invited to stand in the ballroom and be introduced, each in their turn, to their Prince's soon-to-be bride.

Frederick, proud as any peacock, escorted Frances around the huge room. With her hand on Frederick's arm, Frances smiled, nodded, and acknowledged curtsies. She spoke easily, with natural charm; although her voice was lighter and lacked the warmth of Nell's contralto, Frances made a respectable showing.

But Nell, walking just behind Frances's right shoulder, was on tenterhooks the whole time. Even when he wasn't shoulder-to-shoulder with her in the press—a situation that raised tension of a different sort in them both—he sensed her focus, her unrelentingly fixed attention, the way she held herself in expectation of something going wrong . . . but what?

Nell knew better than to imagine that they would escape the soiree without any difficulty, not when Frances's uncertainty had already broken through once. Luckily, Frances managed to hold the whispers at bay through most of the event, and indeed, guests were starting to leave and the crowd about them was thinning before the problem resurfaced and Frances's confidence wavered, then fell.

With, finally, no one left to greet, Frederick turned to Frances and smiled. "Perhaps, now, we can stroll on our own and speak privately, liebchen."

And suddenly Frances was breathless. "Yes—no! That is . . ." Attempting to draw her fingers from Frederick's, wide—wild—eyed, Frances glanced around.

Nell stepped in, closer, using her body to

physically block any move the slighter Frances might have made; heavens above, she could not bolt. Could not be allowed to, not here, not now, not ever. Sliding a supportive—anchoring—arm around her sister's waist, Nell spoke to Frederick. "Your Highness, I regret to say my sister is dreadfully tired. What with the long journey and the subsequent full round of engagements, she's sorely in need of a good night's rest."

Frederick was instantly contrite. "Of course, dear Lady Cornelia." He looked at Frances, then gently, if awkwardly, patted her hand. "My dear, I am full of apologies—it has, indeed, been such an unrelentingly busy day for you. We should have been more considerate."

With Nell's arm tightening around her, Frances rallied. Lifting her head, she managed a wan smile. "No—it's I who am full of apologies, sir. But I fear my sister is correct—I am wilting and in dire need of rest, and would like, with your permission, to retire."

"Of course, my dear. Of course." Frederick raised Frances's fingers to his lips, then bowed gallantly and released her. "Sweet dreams, liebchen —we will meet again in the morning."

Frances curtsied, as did Nell, then Nell looped her arm in Frances's and together the sisters turned and left the now largely empty ballroom.

Standing beside Frederick, Robert watched them go—watched Nell's head tip toward Frances's. It was Nell who was speaking to Frances, while all Frances did was nod.

"Is anything amiss, do you think?"

Robert glanced up to see Frederick, puzzled, frowning slightly at the pair.

"Have we not done something we should, perhaps? Or have we been too demanding—"

"It's not that—nothing like that." Robert clapped him on the arm; Nell's earlier words—that Frederick might have concerns or questions—echoed in his head. "It's tiredness and, at most, just nerves. Don't worry."

Frederick's frown lightened, but didn't leave his eyes. "If you do learn that there is some problem, you will tell me, nein?"

"Of course. But trust me, there's nothing that's going to come between you and Frances and your appointment before the altar in six days' time." Of that, Robert was quite certain.

It was his job to make sure of it.

𝒯o Nell's relief, Frances woke the next morning with renewed enthusiasm and no hint of any lingering nerves. That, of course, wouldn't last, but Nell was ready to accept whatever boons fate

granted her. Over breakfast, they learned that a
tour of the town had been arranged for that morning; duly fortified, they met Frederick and Robert
in the front hall, and left the palace in an open
carriage with an escort of six mounted soldiers,
more, Frederick assured Frances, for ceremonial
show than out of any need for protection.

With Robert's presence on the bench seat
beside her once more pressing on her senses and
her mind, Nell determinedly distracted herself
by looking around at the neat squares, the well-
tended houses, and the cheery flowers in window
boxes hanging over the cobbled streets, while simultaneously keeping an ear on the conversation
between Frederick and Frances, who were sharing the forward-facing seat.

The weather remained gloriously fine, and
Frances's mood continued in similar vein through
the various organized halts. The first was at the
Rathaus, the town hall, where they were wel-
comed by the mayor, bedecked in his robes and
weighted down by gold chains, and a bevy of al-
dermen. Nell, hanging back in Frances's shadow,
was pleased by how graciously her sister dealt
with the gentlemen—but then, in her usual state,
Frances was customarily serenely assured.

After partaking of refreshments and chatting
amiably, they departed for the town marketplace.

There they walked among the populace—a delightful detour that had Frances laughing, setting Frederick beaming at the silvery sound. From the market square, they walked along a route lined with the town's best shops, a diversion guaranteed to absorb Frances. She grew animated; there was so much to see and enjoy, and she openly shared her delight with Frederick.

So well were matters progressing that Nell started to wonder if, perhaps, the family failing had struck, but was now loosening its grip on her sister, even waning. She could only hope.

Robert had been striding along beside her, silent and far too observant for her liking. As ever, she was intensely aware of him physically filling the space next to her. For some irritating reason, her susceptibility to that awareness hadn't died; she'd fully expected it would have after nine years of starvation. Refocusing on the couple ahead of them, she asked, "What's next?"

"The cathedral. I thought it might be helpful for Frances to see the place before the wedding."

Nell wasn't sure how to respond. Yes, it might be helpful—but then again, it might not.

Robert's gaze hadn't left her face. "Is that all right? I know you went through the rehearsals in London, but walking into a large and overwhelm-

ingly ornate space for the first time . . . I thought
she might prefer it see it first."

Nell forced herself to nod. "It's a good idea."
And it was. She just had to hope there would be
no unintended consequences.

The street they were walking along led into
the cathedral square. An imposing, richly ornate
stone edifice with a tall spire topped with a cross,
the cathedral towered over the town, but was in
turn overlooked by the castle, visible atop the hill
behind the church.

The prelate and his deacons were waiting at the
top of the steps before the carved wooden doors.
Frederick led Frances up and introduced her. The
prelate, a white-haired ancient, exuded kindness
as he patted Frances's hand.

Nell watched closely, surreptitiously sighing
with relief when she detected no stiffening in
Frances.

Robert dragged his attention from Nell long
enough to greet the prelate and introduce her.
She responded with her usual calm composure;
she was one of those females who could simultaneously do several things at once and perform
well on all fronts. She was tracking Frances like
a terrier, alert to every little nuance of her sister's
mood, but she exchanged greetings with the prel-

ate and even made him smile without giving any hint at all that she was concerned about Frances.

But she was concerned. Increasingly, Robert sensed that. And increasingly, he was determined to get to the bottom of it.

Turning, the prelate invited their party to follow him inside. They all did, pausing in the dim foyer to listen as one of the deacons related the history of the church. Then the prelate made a sweeping gesture, inviting them to follow him down the aisle. Frederick, with Frances on his arm, set out in the prelate's wake.

Abruptly, Frances drew back. She made a small sound, then blindly turned away.

And Nell was there. She'd all but leapt forward to come up by Frances's side, catching her sister—trapping her sister?—with one arm around her waist. "Actually"—Nell spoke over Frances's head, which was turned away so no one there could see, to Frederick—"it's thought by many in our family to be . . . possibly unlucky to walk down the aisle with one's groom before the wedding." With a gesture, Nell waved at the other aisle that led down the side of the church. "Perhaps we could walk down the side aisles, and"—she beamed at the deacon who had delivered the history lecture—"we might hear more about the church's history as we go."

Despite having no idea what was going on, Robert stepped up in support. "That's an excellent idea." For the prelate and the deacons, he added, "We'll see more of the church that way."

There was a second's pause as everyone looked at Frederick.

"Ah, I see." Although he looked a trifle uncertain and worried, Frederick nodded. "A wedding superstition. This is understandable and must be accommodated."

Nell smiled encouragingly at Frederick. She eased her hold on Frances, who straightened; Nell determinedly wound her arm in Frances's and started strolling toward the ornate chapel to the side of the foyer. Frederick fell in beside Frances, ducking his head to see her face.

Walking behind the trio, Robert saw Nell's arm tighten, then Frances raised her head and said something to Frederick, who smiled and straightened, transparently relieved.

By the time they'd walked down the side aisle and reached the main altar, all was well again. Frances might be a trifle quieter than before, but she seemed completely composed and attentive. She complimented the prelate very prettily on the magnificence of the altar, then she, Nell, and the prelate discussed the relevant positioning to be used during the wedding service.

Robert glanced at Frederick and saw him nodding as he followed the conversation. His friend appeared reassured by Frances's increasing animation.

All Robert had were increasingly urgent questions, but it wasn't Frances he needed to interrogate.

But he got no chance to isolate Nell. Once they'd finished their tour of the cathedral it was time to return to the castle for a private and more relaxed family lunch. Following Nell, Frances, and Frederick into the family dining room, and finding both sets of parents and Frederick's uncles and aunts already present, Robert put aside any thought of pursuing his questions immediately; he would have to bide his time.

$\mathscr{H}$e thought his time had come when, after the meal was concluded, Frederick suggested a walk in the gardens and Frances, after a momentary hesitation during which she'd glanced at Nell, accepted.

Robert would have preferred to take Nell elsewhere, preferably somewhere he could sit her down and watch her face while he asked his questions and demanded answers, but as everyone clearly expected her to act as chaperon, he fell in with good grace by her side. With Frances on his arm, Frederick led the way out of the terrace doors, across the paved terrace, and down the steps to the parterre.

Pacing alongside Nell as she followed, Robert expected her to slow, to allow the betrothed, shortly-to-be-married couple to draw ahead and have some degree of privacy, affording him and her the same, but instead Nell remained ferociously focused on the pair, allowing them to get no more than ten feet ahead.

Given the questions he wished to ply her with, he needed greater privacy; he slowed his pace, expecting her to do the same, but she continued to forge on, leaving him behind.

Exasperated, he lengthened his stride and caught up with her. "Slow down—I want to speak with you."

"Not now." She glanced at him, briefly searched his eyes; he thought she might have sighed. "Later." She looked at the couple ahead. "Trust me—not now."

Trust her? About what? And why not now?

They turned down a walk shaded by sculpted shrubbery. Ahead of them, Frederick and Frances strolled on. Nell's focus on the couple was so blinkered, so compelling, Robert followed her gaze and looked, too . . . and saw the hesitancy that had crept into Frances's manner. There was no one thing that screamed uncertainty, but rather her whole stance, the way she held her head, no longer high and assured but lowered, as if she were trying to calm herself—and failing—set his inner alarms ringing.

Frances slowed. So did Frederick. Looking down at his bride-to-be, concern filled his face. "Liebchen?"

Robert all but heard the breath Frances gulped in, then she drew her hand from Frederick's sleeve and started to turn away.

Before Frances had accomplished a quarter-turn, Nell had sped up and was there. Sliding an arm about her sister's waist, she masked Frances's turn with a wave and the words, "Isn't that the most wonderful magnolia? It's just like the one we have at home, isn't it?" thus disguising Frances's movement as a wish to point out the large flowering tree to Frederick.

Frederick blinked, then raised his gaze to the tree. "I see." After a moment, he drew breath and looked down into Frances's face. He smiled gently. "It is good that you have something to remind you of your home. Does your tree flower as well?"

Frances tipped her head, then studied the tree anew. "I believe this tree is bigger—older. It has more branches, so more flowers, I think."

"We should look to see what else there is here that's reminiscent of home." Nell cast a glance at Robert, faintly wide eyes imploring his aid.

His diplomatic mask in place, he waved ahead. "If we go on a little further, there are some elders. As I recall you have lots of elders around your family's country house."

The rest of their walk transformed into a ramble, one filled with spotting familiar plants. Although led by Nell, with Robert in support, both Frederick and Frances were eventually drawn into the game, and in the end, the betrothed couple were once again at ease and laughing together.

Robert glanced at Nell as, at last, she fell back to stroll alongside him. He could almost feel her exhausted relief. When, sensing his gaze, she glanced up at him, he caught her dark eyes and said just one word. "Later."

She sighed quite audibly, nodded, and faced forward.

Looking ahead, too, hands clasped behind his back, he continued to pace beside her.

"*F*our more *days!*" Nell sprawled in an armchair in the sitting room of the suite her parents had been given. "Neither I nor Frances will survive."

"Don't be melodramatic, dear—it's so unlike

you." In the other armchair, Valeria settled a gauzy shawl about her shoulders. "Besides, it's hardly a matter of survival. Merely of managing, and you, darling, are very good at that."

"Flattery, Mama, will, in this instance, advance your cause not at all. I'm exhausted."

Valeria sighed. "So what stage has poor Frances reached?"

"I had to step in twice today and stop her from . . . Well, I suspect if I hadn't interfered, she would have fled the scene."

"Oh, dear." Valeria looked more worried than she had. "That is troubling."

"Yes. Especially as—as aforesaid—we still have four more days to 'manage.' " Nell sighed. "And there's more, which is really why I'm here. Robert knows—oh, not the reason, but after today he's not going to rest until he has an explanation, and I fear Frederick's . . . a little more than curious. Suspicious, in fact." She met her mother's eyes. "So what should I do?"

They were in the hiatus between coming inside and dressing for dinner; Valeria had changed her gown, but had yet to have her maid put up her fair hair, or don her jewels. Nell watched her mother frown as she digested the news.

"Where is poor Frances?" Valeria eventually asked.

"I left her lying down in her room. She's mortified, of course, but I hope I've convinced her that as yet we've concealed the attacks well enough to pass—well, at least to all others except Robert and Frederick."

"And the attacks themselves?"

Nell sighed. "They seem more acute than either she or I expected."

Valeria grimaced. "Well, then, given, as you keep pointing out, we have four more days before the wedding, I believe we have no option other than to confide in dear Robert, and also Frederick. Perhaps if you speak to Robert and explain, he can pass the information on to Frederick in the most appropriate way."

"Hmm. I gather Robert considers seeing this wedding to a successful conclusion as vital to furthering his career."

"Very likely. You know how competitive the Knightley boys are about their efforts for the crown in foreign climes. I gather that since the Corsican upstart's fall, the family has gone from strength to strength in the Foreign Office. I know your father was told very favorable things about Robert before we came."

Nell arched her brows. "He was always observant and clever."

"Indeed. So I counsel you to see him and explain as required—and I see no point in hiding anything from him. He can then decide how much to reveal, and how, to his friend."

"Very well—that will solve that issue. But do you know of any way to"—Nell gestured—"*ameliorate* these attacks? If they grow more frequent, we'll have the devil of a time concealing them."

Valeria compressed her lips as she thought, then she looked at Nell. "Distraction. If she's thinking and doing other things, she can't be panicking, so fill her day—from morn to night—as much as you possibly can. Have her engaged with something interesting every single hour—I gather that worked for Selena, my cousin's daughter."

Nell frowned. "What sort of things—"

"The same things you would find interesting and engaging—Frances and you are very much alike, after all. Felicity and Esme are similar, and you and Frances share many traits—I've often noted it."

Nell arched her brows, but then nodded. "Thinking of it, yes, I daresay you're right. So . . ."

"So once you've explained all to dear Robert, tell him what we believe we need to do to help Frances through these next days and ask for his help, and his advice." Valeria smiled. "I find it's always helpful to have a solution ready to hand when one explains a problem to a gentleman—and asking for his help is a sure way to bringing him around. Men love to be thought helpful, and if you can make him feel like a savior, so much the better."

Nell laughed and stood. "You're incorrigible, Mama."

"Of course." Valeria held up her face for Nell to kiss. "But I'm right nevertheless. You'll see."

"Very well—I'll engage to put your sage counsel to the test. I'll arrange to meet with Robert later tonight."

*N*ell didn't have to arrange to meet with Robert. After another near-disaster in the drawing room after dinner, which she barely managed to contain and adequately disguise, when everyone else retired, drifting out through the drawing room's double doors and up the main stairs, Robert was waiting just inside the doors. He didn't just catch her eye as, feeling harried and even more exhausted, having consigned an inwardly shaken Frances to Valeria's care, Nell brought up the rear of the crowd; as she drew level with him, Robert reached out and caught her arm.

It was the first time they'd touched in nine years. The jolt to her pulse was stunning.

He paused, as if feeling it, too, then gentled his grip. For a moment, his eyes searched hers, then his lips thinned. "I'd like a word, if I may. In private."

She nodded. "Where?"

Releasing her, he led her upstairs to his study. It was a masculine room, all dark brown leather and polished wood. Eschewing the cluttered desk, Nell made for the armchairs angled before the empty fireplace. Sinking into one, she watched as Robert closed the door, then came to stand before the hearth.

Robert looked down at her, and asked the question she clearly expected to be asked. "What's going on?"

She looked up at him for a moment, then stated, "Nothing that should impact the wedding itself. Rather . . . it's a situation we—you and I—need to manage, one that will end with the dawn four days hence."

He blinked, calculated. "On their wedding day?"

She nodded.

When she didn't say more, he arched a brow. "Nerves?"

Her lips twisted. "Of a sort. I'm thinking of how best to put it—to explain it so that you'll understand."

"Just tell me."

She sighed. "Very well—Frances has proved to be subject to the Vayne family failing. We didn't know if she would be, although the chances were good that she would, given no other female in the family has escaped the curse to date."

"Curse? What curse?"

She gestured. "You've seen it—the sudden inexplicable panics. That's the Vayne family failing in action. More than anything else, that's why I had to be here—because one of us who understands and can remain with her at all times needed to be here to . . . stop her. Shepherd her and steer her out of it. Stop her from bolting if that's how the failing struck."

Blinking, feeling very much like shaking his head in disbelief, Robert shifted and sank into the armchair facing her. "Vayne—that's your mother's family, isn't it?"

Nell nodded. "That's where the failing comes from."

"And this failing can take different forms?"

Again she nodded. "With different ladies. For instance, Mama actually bolted. The day before their wedding, she got in a gig and was driving herself out of London when Papa caught up with her. But she'd felt no panic until that day. Luckily, Papa wasn't the self-effacing sort—he raced straight after her, which, as it happens, was the right thing to do. Mama had no idea where she was going, or even why—she just panicked."

"So . . . if Frances bolts, Frederick has to go after her?"

"One of us will need to, but I'm hoping it won't come to that."

He felt . . . disorientated.

"Felicity, now, had three days of attacks to weather, but they were relatively mild. She just got in a flustered dither and made no sense, but that wasn't hard to gloss over. Esme, like Mama, only had one attack and that on the day before the wedding, but we were ready and no one believed her wedding gown had suddenly been torn and stained beyond redemption. Once she snapped out of it, Esme didn't have a clue why she'd thought that."

"This . . . ah, curse. It doesn't last into the wedding day?"

"It never has, and that's from experience of many weddings, my mother's sisters and their cousins and my cousins—all the females with Vayne blood. For some reason, once we get to the day itself, the curse vanishes."

"Never to return?"

"Never to return in any form."

Relief washed through him. "Having encouraged and facilitated this match, that's comforting to know."

"I daresay. With Frances, we didn't know if, or when, or even in what form the curse would strike. Sadly, it first manifested on the barge, six full days before the wedding. And you've seen what it's like—she draws back, pulls back. But— and this is the critically important part—her reactions have nothing to do with her feelings, or what she truly wants. She's horrified when she snaps out of it, but while the panic is on her, she's not actually thinking at all. Frances is very much in love with Frederick, and she very definitely wants to marry him—the panic attacks don't in any way reflect or alter her feelings."

"Hmm." He frowned. "So we could characterize these attacks as an extreme case of bridal nerves and nothing more."

Nell nodded. "We could." She smoothed one hand along the arm of the chair. "Mama and I suspect that, in the circumstances, and with four days still to go, we need to explain at least some of this to Frederick. He's already noticed, and he must be wondering."

"He is." Robert met her eyes as she glanced up. When she arched her brows, he hesitated, then nodded. "All right. I'll speak with him and make sure he understands. Which leads to my next question, which will also be Frederick's next question—how should he behave during these attacks?"

"Essentially as my father did. Frederick won't be able to ignore the attacks, but he absolutely mustn't react to them by drawing back himself. That only gives the attacks a sort of internal credence, and will most likely make things worse. He needs to stand firm and not let Frances physically pull away. If he accepts that the attack is happening, but that it's nonsensical and irrelevant and will be over soon, and simply smiles, nods, speaks soothingly, and goes on as if the attack hasn't happened, that's the surest way to snap Frances out of it, and all will be well."

Robert spent some moments digesting that, then nodded. "All right. As Frederick is deeply attached to Frances, I don't foresee any problem in enlisting his aid, especially as this is purely a case of temporary and understandable nervy panics." He saw Nell's lips twitch upward, and permitted himself a self-deprecating smile; he was, indeed, already framing the situation in diplomatic language. "Let's assume we—me, you, and Frederick—are all apprised and acting in concert. I assume we can count on your parents if need be?"

"Yes, but they will only be with us during the evening events."

"Indeed. So is there anything we can do to . . . avoid the attacks, or minimize their severity?"

"We—Mama and I—think distraction might work. If we can fill Frances's days with events that keep her actively engaged and entertained, we believe that will reduce the scope for an attack."

He nodded. "That has a certain logic. What events are most likely to engage her interest?"

"As Mama reminded me, Frances and I are much alike, so what would work for me . . ."

Frances and I are much alike. Robert's brain seized on the words, focused on them—and their implications. All of him stilled. The Vayne family failing had manifested in Frances as a pulling back, a drawing back from the man she loved, even though she loved him and wanted to marry him. Frances's attacks had started earlier, further ahead of the wedding, than her family had expected. And no Vayne lady had ever escaped the curse.

Nell was as much of a Vayne as Frances. And Nell and Frances were much alike in many ways . . .

While Nell sat in the chair and talked, listing various excursions and events she felt would provide suitable distraction, and some part of his mind listened and cataloged, and he nodded every now and then, most of his mind, certainly all of his attention, followed her earlier revelations to the inescapable conclusion . . .

A conclusion that rocked him. That shattered his perceptions of their past, and reformed them.

Leaving him with a new and novel perspective.

A much more accurate view of how things had been.

Dragging a breath into lungs suddenly tight, he refocused on Nell.

To discover her looking at him quizzically.

His mind caught up with her words; he nodded. "We can arrange most of that, and yes, I think we should." Rising, he crossed to the desk, found a sheet of paper and a pencil, picked up a ledger for her to use as a support, and returned to her. He handed her the items. "Let's make a list."

While she settled the ledger on the chair arm, smoothed out the paper and lifted the pencil, he sat, and ruthlessly forced his mind to the matter at hand. "Let's do it day by day, and crowd as much into each day as we can."

Eyes on her list, she nodded. "So—tomorrow."

"*Well!*" Nell let herself fall into the armchair in Robert's study. "That went better than I'd dared hope. One attack only, and that relatively minor— and I have to compliment you. Whatever you told

Frederick, however you phrased it, must have been exactly right. He came up trumps, and you may pass on from me that he isn't doing himself any harm at all in Frances's eyes."

Smiling, Robert came to sit in the other arm-chair. "I'll let him know. He was quite nervous, although I know it didn't show. But he did, indeed, hold the line admirably."

He'd brought their list of events, now super-imposed on the affianced couple's official sched-ule. It was presently mid afternoon, and he'd suggested they seize the half an hour between their last event—a viewing of the castle's stables and kennels—and a formal afternoon tea to be attended by all the young ladies of the court to review their upcoming arrangements. He pe-rused the revised schedule. "After this tea—and if Frances is immersed and entertained, we can extend the event until half an hour before the dressing gong—then we have the formal draw-ing room and dinner with all the ambassadors." He glanced at Nell. "I'll do my best to keep the ambassadors and envoys circling, but several are pompous old windbags, so be prepared to step in and divert any who linger too long. A few—the Russian envoy, for one, and the French ambas-sador almost certainly—will attempt to monopo-lize our pair. While Frederick won't need to leave

Frances's side, it would be best if between us, we—you and I, because your parents will be fully engaged themselves—try to ensure one of us is there to back Frederick up at any time."

He grimaced. "I have this persistent vision of one of the ambassadors deciding to buttonhole Frederick and draw him aside while I'm not by to stop it, effectively forcing Frederick to leave Frances standing there alone."

Nell frowned. "What about the wives? They'll be there, won't they?"

"Yes, but they don't generally come forward. At these sort of events they usually gather like a flock of geese and sit and cackle at one end of the room."

"With a new and shiny princess-to-be in their midst?" Nell threw him a look. "Leave it to me— and Mama. We'll have them with their gloved hands on their husbands' arms, sticking like glue to get as much time as they can with Frances. As they'll be intent on her and Frederick in a personal sense, and not interested in anything political, I should think their presence will restrict their spouses' ability to turn the conversation to political affairs."

He widened his eyes. "I hadn't thought of that, but you might well be right." He nodded. "I'll leave the wives to you."

Raising the schedule, he studied the following events. "After dinner, there'll be dancing in the ballroom."

"That will be no problem at all—Frances loves to dance, and as I recall so does Frederick."

Robert nodded. "So with luck we'll weather tonight well enough, and then tomorrow we have the visit to the orphanage, and then the guilds' luncheon at the Rathaus, and after that we've slotted in visits to a weaving factory, then the silk merchants' warehouse, and last but not least, to the crown jewelers." He glanced up. "That's going to be quite a day."

Nell nodded happily. "Yes, it is, and the curse is going to have to fight for an opening. Excellent!" She rose and shook out her skirts.

Rising, too, Robert laid aside the list and just looked at her for a moment—a rare moment when she wasn't looking at him.

Then she looked up and met his eyes. Searched them, then said, "It's time I fetched Frances and Mama for the tea."

He smiled. "Indeed." He waved her to the door. "I'll go downstairs and make sure all's in readiness."

He followed her out of the study and they parted, each to do their part in managing the Vayne family failing.

𝒯he following day, they maneuvered to sit alongside each other at the end of one table at the luncheon the town's guild masters hosted to toast the royal bride and groom.

When the speeches got under way, at the center of the high table Frances sat, apparently rapt, alongside Frederick, whose protective tendencies had only grown more marked with every passing hour, especially as Frances seemed to be increasingly leaning on him to help her through her panicky flutters. Which, Nell felt, was an unexpected boon.

Satisfied her sister was as well-guarded as she might be, when Robert drew a sheet of paper from his pocket, unfolded it, and smoothed it out, Nell readily consented to turn her attention to their plans for the afternoon.

Having realized that she had an excellent memory for names, Robert duly filled her in as to whom they would meet that afternoon at the weaving factory, the silk warehouse, and the jewelers. "I estimate we'll get back to the castle only just in time to change for dinner. It's a family dinner tonight—only Frederick's immediate family and yours."

"Good." Nell sat back and met Robert's eyes. Steady gray eyes, stubborn square chin. He was as she remembered him, but with depth, or was it new facets? No—more like previously hidden depths that were now more discernible. She smiled. "We've done very well so far. Especially this morning. The orphanage was fun—I think they can be certain that Frances will want to become their patron."

Relaxing in his chair, Robert smiled back, and wondered if she had any idea how revealing her interest in the children at the orphanage had been. Although Frances had certainly been interested, too, she had largely followed in Nell's shadow. In truth, it was Nell who truly commanded the innate graciousness associated with a duke's daughter; she had just the right touch, leaving those she dealt with feeling honored, without in any way making an issue of her status.

Nell's gaze had drifted back to the guild master currently at the podium, leaving him free to let his gaze rest on her, to let his mind dwell on what he'd finally understood about the unraveling of their romance long ago.

As his gaze traced her face, he felt the determination to make a bid, again, for the only lady he'd ever wanted as his own well and harden.

"There you are, my dears." Valeria drifted up, setting a languid hand on Nell's and Robert's shoulders. She smiled at Nell as Nell glanced up, then, as Nell returned her gaze to the speaker, Valeria met Robert's gaze. And nodded. "You're doing very well."

With a pat on his shoulder, Valeria drifted on.

Robert blinked, looked again at Nell, and wondered at the ambiguity he'd detected in her mother's words.

"*O*ne more day." Perched sidesaddle on a sweet black mare, Nell cantered alongside Robert, mounted on a raking gray. She nodded ahead to where Frances and Frederick were bowling along in a gig, with Frederick teaching Frances to manage the ribbons. "Teaching Frances to drive was an inspired notion. With luck, that will keep her entirely engrossed on the drive out, and the drive home again. And what with the lunch at the hunting lodge, then the visit to the farm, while I hardly dare to suggest it, we might reach tonight —or to be more precise, tomorrow's dawn— without major incident."

"The dinners tonight are private and separate," Robert said. "Your family at one, and Frederick's at another. No real likelihood of any untoward occurrence there, so once we get back to the castle this afternoon—"

"Oh, no—I'm not counting my chickens until

tonight, until Frances retreats into her bedchamber and closes the door."

Robert grinned. His gaze returned to Frances. They'd let the gig draw ahead. "She's only had three minor episodes since we started our campaign of distraction, and Frederick's managed all three by himself."

"He's been more sympathetic than I expected him to be." Nell's gaze, too, dwelled on Frederick's and Frances's heads. "I feel even more confident than I was before that they'll truly have a wonderful marriage."

Robert made no reply, not that she'd expected one. About them, the morning had waxed warm, but a breeze off the river kept temperatures pleasant. Birds trilled and swooped in the hedgerows they passed, and the rich scent of grain ripening in the sun teased their senses.

"There's a lookout on that ridge ahead. They can't reach it in the gig—but we can." Robert met her gaze as she glanced at him. "You said it yourself—Frances is unlikely to have any difficulty while she's concentrating so hard on learning to drive." Tipping his head toward the ridge, he smiled, unvoiced challenge in his eyes. "We can ride down the other side and rejoin the party, and the view from up there is said to be the best in Lautenberg."

She laughed. "All right. I can see you're searching for a reason to let your mount stretch his legs." She waved. "Lead on."

Robert drew aside, spoke briefly to the captain of the honor guard of six riders following their Prince, then he urged his gray away and down a narrow track; perched on her black, Nell followed.

Once off the road, they let their mounts stretch into an easy gallop. The track they were following led into a forest; they slowed as, now a narrower bridle path, the track climbed the ridge in a series of switchbacks.

Eventually, they reached the top of the ridge and Robert led the way over and into the wide clearing carved out on the side of the hill. Before them, lush green fields stretched to either side, to the distant blue line of the Mosel on their right, and all the way to the cloud-hazed mountains that marked the border with Luxembourg to the left.

He reined in and Nell halted her mare beside his gray. She looked out, eagerly scanning. Her cheeks were rosy, her lips lush and ripe, her large, dark-pansy eyes bright with eager interest. He considered the sight, then swung down from the saddle.

She looked at him questioningly as he came to lift her down.

"We can sit for a little while. The road will take them around and over a pass—it'll be some time before they reach the stretch below us."

Her lips formed an "oh" and she slid her boots free, then allowed him to close his hands about her waist and swing her down.

She lost her breath. He was watching, so saw it, but pretended he hadn't.

Releasing her, he waved to the view. "Come—I'll point out the sights."

She didn't attempt any verbal response, just nodded and walked beside him to the edge of the cliff.

He started at the Mosel, and she was quickly pointing to landmarks and asking about the smaller towns and villages they could see nestling in the landscape. When eventually he'd named or explained all that they could see, she sighed. "It's really very peaceful here—much less noisy and crowded and bustling than London, but oddly the countryside seems more . . . alive somehow." She glanced at him. "The country here is different from the countryside at home."

He nodded. "Here there's less large-estate farming and more of other crafts, like woodworking, and metal crafting, and jewelry making, cloth making, and animal husbandry of many more types. The villages are a lot closer—to walk from one to the next would take less than an hour—so it's easier for the villagers and towns-folk to barter and trade . . ." He grimaced lightly. "I suppose the main difference is that there are no major landowners other than the royal family, so most people in Lautenberg have at least their own small patch to raise grain, or chickens, or build a forge and sell their wares."

"They're all independent?"

"They pay taxes to the royal family, but those aren't onerous and go primarily to keeping the various necessary arms of the government opera-tional." His lips twisted cynically. "As the British envoy, I'm not sure saying so isn't a form of trea-son, but I prefer the peace and tranquility, and, yes, the relative equality of this place."

He felt her gaze on his face. "Will you stay here, then? Even when you're no longer the envoy?"

He shrugged. "Perhaps." He looked at her. "It depends." He let a moment tick past, then asked, "What of you?" With a wave, he directed her gaze back to the vista spread before them. "If you could, would you live here, surrounded by this brand of peace and harmony, with Frances near . . . or would you rather the bustle of London, and the quieter space of a large estate in the English countryside?"

She gazed out, considering, then her lips lightly

curved. "If I could . . . strangely enough, I can see myself here, which is not at all what I'd expected. Lautenberg is . . . human-sized in a way larger countries are not."

"Aptly put." He didn't give her time to dwell further on his question, but waved her to the horses. "We should start down. The gig should have cleared the pass by now—it'll be coming along the road below us shortly."

Nell filled her lungs one more time with the sweetly scented air, then exhaled, turned, and walked back to the mare. And steeled her nerves, her senses, against the rush of feeling as Robert's hands slid about her waist and gripped, and he lifted her—so effortlessly—to her saddle.

Her lungs seized again, but she'd expected that; she didn't let it ruffle her but used the moment while he walked to his horse and mounted to settle her boots in the stirrups and arrange her riding skirt, then lifting her head—finding him looking directly at her—she smiled and nodded at him to lead the way down.

As she followed him slowly down what proved to be a steeper track on this side of the ridge, she had ample time to let her gaze travel over his well-shaped head, his shoulders, and the long length of his back. He cut a dashing figure atop the heavy gelding, and managed the powerful animal with negligent ease. After nine years with no real contact, it seemed strange to have fallen so easily into the same relaxed rapport they'd previously shared; he was the only man she'd ever felt so at ease with, so free to simply indulge and enjoy his company.

She'd always regretted the fact that he'd drawn back, that he hadn't made an offer for her hand, and, now she thought of it, she had to own to considerable surprise to find him still unwed. He was a Knightley; his family were diplomats, one and all, and, in general, diplomats were expected to marry, to have a helpmate in their duties.

She tried to imagine what his wife would be like, when he finally chose her. She imagined several young English ladies she knew, measured them against the role, yet none seemed at all suitable; none found favor in her eyes. Then again, she was only an old friend, and a long distant one at that; he might have changed significantly since they'd been close . . . only she didn't think he had.

He was older, yet so much about him seemed achingly familiar. She'd had to steel her heart against the temptation to dwell on all she'd missed, on all she'd not had to enjoy for the past nine years . . . she wished she knew why he'd never asked for her hand. Wished she knew what she'd done wrong, what she'd done to make him step back when she'd thought he was about to step closer, close enough to take her in his arms . . .

With an irritated shake of her head, she banished the useless, repetitive meanderings. She was here, now, with him, and at least for the next several hours, she could take pleasure in his company.

He drew rein as they reached the road; as she halted her mare alongside his gray, she could hear the rattle of the gig's wheels drawing nearer.

She turned to him. "Will you be dining with us tonight? Or are you expected to dine with Frederick?"

His lips twisted. "Frederick's family will expect me, I fear, but . . ." Robert met her eyes. "Why don't we meet in my study later—once you've seen Frances to her bedchamber and can report, absolutely, that our campaign has reached a successful conclusion?"

Nell grinned. "Yes. All right."

The gig rounded the nearby corner and the rattle of its wheels cut off any further conversation.

Not that Robert wished to say anything more; he was more than satisfied with what he'd achieved.

$\mathcal{I}$t was just after eleven o'clock when Nell finally made her way down the corridor to Robert's study door. A line of lamplight showed beneath the door; feeling more lighthearted, freer than she had for weeks and weeks, she tapped lightly, then opened the door and swept in.

Robert was seated at his desk; he'd been reading some papers. The lamp on one corner shed strong light over the desk, striking deep red glints from his dark brown hair. He'd looked up as she entered; smiling, he laid aside the papers and beckoned her nearer. Leaning back in his chair, he reached out and lifted a small bottle of champagne from a bucket of ice, along with two glasses.

"Here." He held out the glasses.

Rounding the desk, she leaned back against one corner and took both glasses, holding them while he eased the stopper from the bottle. It popped and he seized one glass, deftly catching the foaming bubbles that cascaded forth.

He glanced up at her as the froth slowed and he poured bubbly liquid into the glass. "I hope celebrations are in order. I take it Frances has retired and all is well?"

"Yes, she has, and yes." Accepting the filled glass, Nell handed him the other. "I can report that we are, indeed, home and hosed, and the wedding will proceed with no further hiccups or hitches."

"Thank heaven!" His own glass filled, Robert clinked the rim to hers, then raised his glass in a toast. "To the successful conclusion of our campaign."

"Hear, hear!" She lifted her glass in salute, then sipped. "Mmm, that's nice." She looked at the glass, at the bubbles rising within the liquid, then raised the glass again. "To Frances, another Vayne lady who has managed to reach her wedding day without major mishap."

Robert's lips curved, but lightly. His gray gaze remained steady on her face. "To Frances and her wedding."

They both sipped again.

"And," Robert returned, "we shouldn't forget Frederick, who stepped up to the mark in sterling fashion, and in doing so forged an even deeper bond with his soon-to-be bride."

"No, indeed." Nell leaned closer and clinked her glass to Robert's. "We definitely shouldn't forget Frederick."

Robert sipped and watched her swallow a healthy gulp of the champagne, then he reached out and slipped the glass from her fingers.

She blinked as he pushed back his chair, rose, and set both glasses aside. "I hadn't finished."

"I know, but I want you fully compos mentis for what comes next."

She spread her arms. "But my travails are all over."

Shifting to stand before her, he caught her hands and drew her upright. Frowning, she studied his face. "What comes next?"

"Something I've been wanting to do ever since I saw you step onto the deck of the royal barge." Releasing her hands, he raised his, framed her face and tipped it up, and kissed her.

Gently, at first, but then his lips firmed and . . . Nell couldn't catch her breath. Couldn't steady her suddenly reeling head. A sensation like fizz erupted deep inside her and she felt giddy, deliriously whirling—and none of that had anything to do with the champagne.

She responded, not hesitantly as she'd expected, but with a certainty born of some seed that had been planted long ago. Nine years ago.

Sliding her arms over his shoulders, she moved closer, her lips meeting his with equal ardor, with an equivalent wish to explore, to know . . .

The tip of his tongue cruised the seam of her lips, tempting, enticing. Inciting.

They'd kissed, all those years ago, when she'd been nineteen and he twenty-two, but those tentative kisses had been nothing like this.

This . . . was an invitation, simple and blatant and sure. She read that, understood that, instinctively and in every other way. For an instant, she teetered on the cusp, unsure, but then she looked inward—just one second of consideration—and she knew what her answer should be.

This was her one chance—her last chance. Tomorrow was the wedding, and the day after she would leave, and she'd always—always—wanted him.

As a woman wanted a man, she'd yearned for him.

So she parted her lips and invited him in, surrendered her mouth, and gloried as he took. As he claimed and made his that which always had been.

His hands drifted from her face and his arms closed around her and she closed the last inches between his body and hers.

And desire flared.

At some point he steered her through a door into his adjoining bedroom. To his bed.

Later still, they lay together on the white sheets in a tangle of naked limbs, heated skin, and pounding hearts.

Hands shaped, explored, sculpted, possessed.

And passion burned.

Murmured endearments, encouragements, and

soft moans of delight were the only sounds she heard. She was deaf to all else, blind to the world— for her there was only him.

And for him, it seemed, there was only her. Devotion and reverence invested his touch; his focus was absolute and unwavering.

Sensation and feelings and an upsurge of emotion swept her up and carried her on.

Urged her on.

Until they came together in a rush of fire and glory. And the moment was all, and everything and more than she'd dreamed.

And the man in her arms was the man of her dreams—he always had been. Even as cataclysmic sensation stole her breath, stole her mind and overwhelmed her senses, she yet recognized that as indisputable fact.

This was life, this was joy.

This was pleasure unbounded.

Then ecstasy claimed them, wracked them, shattered them, and satiation rolled over them and she knew no more.

*N*ell woke to the gray light of pre-dawn. For a moment, she was disoriented—the room was similar to her own, but not . . . Then on a rush of remembered sensation, she recalled what had happened. The bed beside her was empty, yet the sheets were still warm.

Silence lay over the room.

Raising her head, she searched, and saw Robert standing before the window, staring out. He'd thrown on a robe.

The bed was in complete disarray; detaching the coverlet required little effort. Wrapping the warm folds about her, she walked quietly across and joined him.

He glanced at her as she halted beside him. Looking out at the glimmer of light just edging the eastern horizon, she murmured, "You seduced me. I'm not complaining—I'm glad you did—but now I can think again, I have to wonder why."

Turning her head, she met his gray eyes, the shade softer in the faint morning light.

He held her gaze. "Because I realized it's what I should have done nine years ago."

She frowned.

His tone hardened. "Well, maybe not that precisely, but . . . I want you with me, Nell—here, wherever I'm posted. I've always wanted you and only you. I haven't been a monk over the years we've been apart, but there's never been anyone else—only you." He held a glass of water; he raised it, sipped, then went on, his gaze moving gently over her face, "When you drew back, I tried to find someone else—someone who wanted me. But I could never find any woman to take your place. For me, it seemed only you would do."

She frowned more definitely, her gaze locked with his. "I didn't draw back—you did."

His lips curved, but ruefully. He shook his head. "Stop and think. Are you, or are you not, the oldest girl of your generation on the Vayne family tree?"

She didn't stop frowning. "I am."

"So in the same way you've been watching out for Frances, who was watching out for you? Who thought to watch your behavior? No one. At that time, nine years ago, the Vaynes didn't know whether your generation would be affected, did they? And you hadn't yet become betrothed. But, my darling Nell, you and I were always sympathetic, empathetic, toward each other. You *knew* I was going to ask for your hand . . . and you drew back."

Confusion overwhelmed her frown. "I did?" She honestly didn't think . . . but then Frances and her sisters and all the other Vayne females rarely had much comprehension of what they did while panicking . . . She refocused on his face. "Are you sure?"

She couldn't disguise the hope that colored her

voice. Was that why he'd drawn back, because she had?

His nod was absolute. "Yes. You pulled back. And I didn't know anything about the Vayne family failing. I was twenty-two, and while now I would probably grow suspicious, press, and ask questions, back then . . ." He paused, holding her gaze. "I thought you didn't want me to propose, that you didn't want me as your husband, and that was why you drew back."

"No!" She searched his eyes and didn't doubt his veracity. "I *wanted* to marry you."

Anguish rang beneath her words. Robert captured one of her hands, drew his thumb soothingly over the back. "It doesn't matter, darling Nell, because that was long ago and this, here and now, is where we are." He held her dark gaze, the rich violet only just taking on color as the sun slowly rose. Raising her hand, he pressed a kiss to her knuckles, and spoke to those wonderful eyes. "I've never stopped loving you, and through these last days, as we worked side by side through our campaign, I came to hope that you still loved me."

Her answer came without a heartbeat's hesitation. "I've always loved you. Only you."

"And as I love you in the same, all-consuming fashion, then it's time, don't you think, that we married?" He drew a breath, and it was tight. "And that's the answer to your question—why I seduced you. Because, my darling Nell, you may draw back, fluster and bluster all you like, but this time, I'm not letting you go."

Nell stared at him, then a laugh bubbled up—a happy, joyous laugh—and she had to let it out.

He smiled in return.

Then before she gathered her wits, he went down on one knee and looked up at her, draped in his coverlet with one shoulder bare and her hair cascading in a tousled mane, and said, "Marry me, Nell, and make me the happiest of mortals."

She dropped onto her knees, too, pressing into arms that closed around her, steadying her and holding her, and smiled into his eyes. "My heart is yours, Robert Knightley. I'll marry you and gladly, and I trust that you'll hold me to this vow—to be your wife and stand by your side forevermore." Then she leaned in and kissed him.

And he kissed her back.

Minutes later, he rose, lifting her in his arms, and carried her back to the bed.

The wedding of Hereditary Prince Frederick of Lautenberg to Frances Daughtry, daughter of the Duke of Pemberton, went off without a hitch.

Until he'd seen the evidence with his own eyes, Robert had privately questioned the assumption that the Vayne curse would vanish with the day's dawn, but from the first—when he'd glimpsed her going into the private family breakfast—Frances had glowed, happiness and joy and delighted expectation rendering her nothing short of radiant.

Nell, gowned in deep violet satin of a shade that matched her eyes, followed Frances into the room, smiling and laughing at something Frances had said; she transfixed Robert's eyes and attention effortlessly. Even walking in Frances's train, to him, Nell was beyond compare.

Throughout the long day, he and she consulted frequently, working through an extensive list of items to be tweaked and last-minute matters to confirm.

As in any major diplomatic event, adjustments had to be made due to unforeseen happenings— like the elderly Grand Duchess of Bavaria, being unable to stand and so unable to see from her allotted perch in the gallery, having to be accommodated nearer the altar—but between them he and Nell rose to the challenge, and not a single disturbance marred the day.

Frederick and Frances made a perfect royal couple, the glow in their eyes and investing their expressions whenever they looked on each other clear for all to see. The populace of Lautenberg, many of whom had crowded into the streets of Kremunz, roared their approval.

The wedding breakfast passed off without incident, and then it was time for the newlyweds to depart on the royal barge on the first night of a romantic wedding cruise.

All those who could followed the royal couple and their attendant families to the docks, where the barge, suitably bedecked, bobbed on a gentle swell.

Half an hour of laughter, cheers, and a short thank-you speech from Frederick to his assembled countrymen, and the ropes were cast off and the barge eased into the river.

Robert watched the gap widen between the dock and the deck, and finally felt the pressure of the day slide from his shoulders.

Nell, standing beside him, sent one last wave toward her sister and her new husband, then linked her arm in Robert's and heaved a heartfelt sigh. "It's done."

"Indeed." Standing in front of Robert, Valeria turned and considered him and her daughter. "And what about you?"

As ever, her question was ambiguous, but, unruffled, Robert smiled and answered it as his future mama-in-law had intended. "As it happens, Your Grace, I'll be returning to England with your party." Raising his gaze, he included the duke, who had come to stand beside Valeria. "I intend to return to London, at least long enough to marry Nell."

The duke smiled. "Excellent!" He clasped Robert's hand and shook it heartily. "About time." The duke beamed at his daughter.

Valeria looked at Nell expectantly, as did Robert. She was staring at them all, apparently struck dumb. Valeria arched her fine brows. "If she'll have you, I suspect you meant to say."

"No, Your Grace." Meeting Nell's stunned eyes, Robert placed his hand over hers on his sleeve. "Regardless of what she says from now until then, I will meet her before the altar at St. George's. I have no intention of drawing back. Again. I love her, and I know she loves me, and"—raising her hand, he pressed a kiss to her fingers—"once I finally get my ring on her finger, I look forward to a long and happy life side by side."

Valeria looked from him to Nell, then smiled delightedly. "Amen."

July 7, 1826
The Deck of the *Mary and Henry*,
bound for the Rhine, crossing
the English Channel

*T*he wind blew fair and the schooner leapt through the waves. Clutching the rail a little short of the bow, Nell stood with Robert, a comforting shield at her back, and watched the coast of Holland take shape on the horizon.

They were returning to Lautenberg, to what would be their home for the foreseeable future, possibly for the rest of their lives. Robert's masters at the Foreign Office had been beyond delighted to learn of his proposed alliance with the Daughtrys; the reassurance of having a sister to support Frances in her role, and the benefits of having a noble lady of Nell's caliber to assist Robert in the delicate diplomacy predicted to be necessary to keep peace in the region, were considered unparalleled boons. As for Robert's family, they, too, were in alt; he was the last of his brothers to wed, and the family had all but given up hope—a hard thing in a family steeped in diplomatic ways.

Her hair whipped by the wind, the tang of sea spray unrelenting, Nell glanced down at the shiny gold band on her ring finger. The last two weeks had been frenetic, hectic, and filled to the brim, but perhaps because their recent brief engagement was effectively the second time for her, she'd fallen prey to no more than several short bouts of frantic dithering, and they'd been married yesterday in St. George's in a relatively small, family wedding; after Frances's recent extravaganza, that had suited them both.

And now, soon, they would reach the mouth of the Rhine, and transfer to the barge that would be waiting to ferry them along the river and then up the Mosel to Kremunz and its fairy-tale castle.

"A penny for your thoughts."

She smiled and leaned back, nestling her head against Robert's shoulder, crossing her arms over his as they circled her waist and held her securely. "I was just thinking . . . this is very much my dream come true, but I never thought beyond this point." She glanced up and caught his eye. "Beyond the wedding. And now we're here, on the threshold of beyond, and I feel . . . so *excited*, so enthusiastic about what lies ahead."

"About making a life together?"

She nodded. "That, and the challenges of managing whatever comes."

His chin against her head, he was silent for a moment, then he murmured, "Just as long as we're together, as long as I can hold you in my arms, I don't care what fate flings at us."

"Just as long as we're together, we can triumph over anything."

"And as we'll always and forever be together, the future, my love, is *finally* ours."

THE END

And now a sneak peek
at #1 *New York Times* bestselling author
Stephanie Laurens's novels

AND THEN SHE FELL

and

THE LADY RISKS ALL

Available now

An Excerpt from

AND THEN SHE FELL

CHAPTER ONE

APRIL 1837
LONDON

$\mathscr{I}$t was time to dress for what was sure to prove a trying evening. As she climbed the stairs of her parents' house in Upper Brook Street, Henrietta Cynster mentally rehearsed the news she would have to impart to her friend Melinda Wentworth when they met as arranged at Lady Montague's ball.

Henrietta sighed. Reaching her bedroom door, she opened it and halted on the threshold, arrested by the sight of her younger sister, Mary, riffling through the jewelry box on Henrietta's dressing table.

Mary acknowledged Henrietta's arrival with a flick of her eyes and continued pawing through the jumble of chains, earrings, brooches, and beads.

Movement drew Henrietta's attention to the armoire beside her bed. Her maid, Hannah, was lifting out Henrietta's new royal-blue ball gown, simultaneously shooting disapproving glances at Mary's slender back.

Stepping inside, Henrietta shut the door. Like her, Mary was still in her day gown and hadn't yet changed. Curious, she studied Mary's intent expression; the baby of the family, Mary had the single-minded focus of a terrier when it came to anything she wanted. "What are you looking for?"

Mary threw her an impatient glance. Shutting one drawer, she reached for the last, the bottom drawer in the box. "The—*aha*!" Inserting, then withdrawing, her fingers, Mary's face transformed as she held up her find, suspending it between the fingers of both hands. "I was looking for this."

Eyeing the necklace of fine gold links interspersed with polished amethyst beads from which a faceted rose-quartz crystal hung, then noting that Mary's expression now held the satisfaction of a general who'd just learned his troops had captured a vital enemy position, Henrietta waved dismissively. "It's never done anything for me. You're welcome to have it."

Mary's vivid blue eyes swung to Henrietta's face. "I wasn't looking for it for me." Mary held out the necklace. "*You* have to wear it."

The necklace had been gifted to the Cynster girls by a Scottish deity, The Lady, and was supposedly a charm to assist the wearer in finding her true hero, the man by whose side she would live in wedded bliss for the rest of her life. Pragmatic and practical, Henrietta had always had difficulty believing in the necklace's efficacy.

More, in the same pragmatic vein, she'd always considered it was unreasonable to expect that all seven Cynster girls of her generation would find love and happiness in the arms of their true heroes, that it was in the cards that one, at least, would not achieve that outcome, and if that were the case, then the Cynster girl destined to die an old maid would, almost certainly, be her.

As she and Mary were the only two Cynster females of their generation yet unwed, her prediction of her spinster-forever state seemed well on the way to becoming fact. She was already twenty-nine and had never been even vaguely tempted to consider marrying any gentleman. Conversely, no one in their right mind would imagine that twenty-two-year-old Mary, dogged, determined, and unswervingly set on defining and forging her future life, would not achieve her already trenchantly stated goal—namely finding and marrying her hero.

Sliding her shawl from her shoulders, Henrietta shook her head. "I told you—it's never worked for me. You may take it with my blessing. I presume that's what this is about—that you want to use it to find your hero?"

"Yes, exactly." Mary's expression hardened. "But I can't just take it. It doesn't work that way. *You* have to wear it and find your hero first, and then hand it to me just as Angelica handed it to you, and Eliza handed it to Angelica, and Heather handed it to Eliza before that—on the evening of your engagement ball."

Turning to set the shawl on a chair, Henrietta hid a smile—that of an older, more mature sister at her little sister's enthusiastic belief in the charm. "I'm quite sure it's not that specific. There's nothing to say it has to work for us all."

"Yes, there is." There was no mistaking the crisp certainty in Mary's tone; as Henrietta turned back to her, she went on, "I asked Catriona, and she asked The Lady, and it's The Lady's charm, after all. And according to Catriona, The Lady was very clear. The necklace has to go from one to the other of us in the stipulated order. Specifically, the necklace won't work for me if it hasn't already worked for you and you haven't had your engagement ball. So!" Mary drew in a breath and, jaw set, held the necklace out to Henrietta. "You have to wear this. From now until you find your hero—and pray to The Lady and all the gods that that will be soon."

Frowning slightly, Henrietta reached out and reluctantly lifted the necklace from Mary's fingers. Refusing it . . . wasn't really an option. Henrietta might be older, more mature, more experienced socially; she might be taller by nearly a head, and she certainly wasn't any weak-willed miss, but the entire Cynster clan knew that attempting to deny Mary something she'd set her heart on was a fool's endeavor, and that was doubly true if she had a logical argument to bolster her case.

Letting the links slide through her fingers, Henrietta once again studied Mary's face. "Why are you so eager to have the necklace now? You know I've had it since Angelica's engagement ball, and that was nearly eight years ago."

"Precisely." Belligerently, Mary narrowed her eyes back. "So you've had eight years to wear it and find your hero, and instead you've put it in your jewelry box and left it there. That didn't matter while I was still in the schoolroom. Even after I was presented, I wanted to look around myself, so you not wearing the necklace wasn't a problem. But I'm twenty-two now, and I'm ready to take the next step. I want to find my hero forthwith, and start my marriage and set up my own household, and all the rest that comes with marrying. Unlike you, I don't want to spend the next seven or more years doing other things, which means"—Mary jabbed a finger at the necklace—"that you have to wear that now, find your hero, and then pass it on to me. Only once I have the necklace can I get on with my life."

Others might have accepted that at face value, but Henrietta knew her little sister just a little too well. "And . . . ?"

Mary held her gaze, vivid cornflower-blue eyes steady and unyielding.

Henrietta tipped her head, arched her brows, and waited. . . .

"Oh, all right!" Mary flung up her hands in surrender. "*And* I think I might have found my perfect hero, but I need the necklace to be sure. The necklace is supposed to come to me, work for me, and then go to Lucilla, so it seems I'm supposed to wait for the necklace before I decide on my hero, and, well, it would seem to be flying in the face of fate and The Lady to make any final hero-decision *before* I get the necklace, and I have to have it in the proper way." Mary's expression firmed; her eyes bored into Henrietta's. "Which means *you* have to wear it and find your hero first."

Henrietta looked down at the necklace, at the innocent links draped over her hand. And sighed. "All right. I'll wear it tonight."

Mary uttered a whoop of delight.

Henrietta held up a staying hand. "But I don't expect it to work for me, so don't get your hopes up."

Mary laughed and darted in to plant a quick peck on Henrietta's cheek. "Just wear it, sister-mine—that's all I ask. As for it working"—eyes twinkling, Mary swung toward the door—"I'll put my faith in The Lady."

Smiling, Henrietta shook her head.

Mary paused at the door. "Are you joining Mama and me at Lady Hammond's tonight?"

"No—I'm expected at Lady Montague's." Given Henrietta's age, she often attended different events than those to which their mother escorted Mary. "Have fun."

"I will. I'll see you tomorrow." With a wave, Mary went out of the door, shutting it behind her.

Still smiling, the necklace in one hand, Henrietta turned to discover that Hannah had put her new gown back in the armoire and instead laid out a gown of purple silk.

Catching Hannah's gaze as the maid turned from the chest of drawers, a purple-and-gold silk shawl in her hands, Henrietta arched a brow.

Correctly interpreting the gesture, Hannah assured her, "The royal blue won't do, miss, not if you're wearing that." Eyes bright, Hannah nodded at the necklace. "And if you're going out looking for your hero, we want you to look your best."

Henrietta inwardly sighed.

*T*wo hours later, Henrietta joined Mr. and Mrs. Wentworth by the side of Lady Montague's ballroom. After exchanging greetings, they stood and watched the Wentworths' daughter, Melinda, who was dancing a cotillion.

Melinda's partner was the Honorable James Glossup.

It was James's motives in paying court to Melinda that had brought Henrietta there; she found herself studying him, absorbing all that his appearance and his expertise in the dance conveyed, and wondering—as she had for the past several days—why, given his transparent attractiveness and accomplishments, James had taken the tack he had with respect to finding a bride.

Mrs. Wentworth, a short, comfortably rotund lady in brown bombazine, sighed. "It's such a shame—they make *such* a handsome couple."

"Now, now." Mr. Wentworth, a solid, conservatively dressed gentleman, patted his wife's hand where it rested on his sleeve. "There'll be other handsome bucks that'll come sniffing around, and as Mellie's of a mind to find a gentleman who loves her . . . well, I'm just grateful to Miss Cynster for finding out what she has."

Henrietta smiled faintly and quashed an impulse to squirm. She didn't know James well, but he was her brother Simon's closest friend; James had been Simon's groomsman when Simon had married two years ago. Consequently, James's and her paths had crossed at several family functions, but beyond what she'd gathered through his association with Simon, she'd had no reason to look more closely at James.

Until he'd grown so particular in his attentions to Melinda that his intention to offer for her hand could not be doubted. At that point, Melinda, with her parents' approval, had turned to Henrietta for, as they'd termed it, "clarification of James's motives."

From her early twenties, Henrietta had found a calling in assisting her peers, the other young ladies of the haut ton, to discover the answer to the critical question every young lady had of the gentleman who sought her hand: Does he love me, or is there some other reason he wishes to marry me?

It wasn't always easy to tell, or, sometimes,

to discover the true answer. Henrietta, however, born into the powerful Cynster clan, with all the connections and associations that afforded her, had long ago learned the ways of finding out almost anything.

She wasn't a gossip; she rarely told anyone anything they hadn't specifically asked to know. But she'd always been observant, and her acuity had only sharpened with the years, with constant application and the resulting experience.

While mamas, matrons, and chaperons guided their charges through the ton's shoals, acting as matchmakers for those young ladies, Henrietta provided a countering service. Indeed, certain disgruntled gentlemen had labeled her "The Matchbreaker," but to the female half of the haut ton, she was the person young ladies set on marrying for love turned to for reassurance as to their would-be fiancés' matrimonial motivations.

With tonnish sentiment over recent years shifting in favor of love-matches, Henrietta's insights and expertise had been much in demand.

It was entirely possible that her extensive experience was the reason behind the nebulous niggle in her brain, the suspicion that *something* about James Glossup's situation didn't quite fit. But Melinda had asked, and Henrietta now knew, so despite that niggling but irritatingly unspecific reservation, she would oblige and tell her friend the truth.

Watching James turn elegantly with the music, surveying his broad shoulders, his long, lean frame, the ineffable grace with which he moved, his impeccable and stylishly subdued attire and fashionably ruffled brown hair, and the smile of true gentlemanly gentleness he bestowed on Melinda, Henrietta wondered yet again why he'd decided to take the tack he had and marry merely to secure extra funds, rather than searching for some lady to love.

He could, of course, simply be a coward too wary of love to take the risk, yet to Henrietta that explanation didn't ring true.

As an acknowledged wolf of the ton, James had prowled the salons shoulder-to-shoulder with Simon, but since the summer of Simon's marriage two years ago, James had drawn back and been little seen in London, not until the beginning of this Season. Regardless, as one of the Dorsetshire Glossups, one of Viscount Netherfield's grandsons, there were any number of suitable young ladies who would be entirely agreeable to falling in love with him, but instead he'd fixed very quickly on Melinda.

And Melinda was one of Henrietta's friends.

The measure concluded. James bowed; Melinda curtsied, then rose. Melinda glanced toward her parents, saw that Henrietta had arrived and, albeit with due courtesy and smiles, dismissed James, parting from him to thread her way through the crowd.

As Melinda drew near, Henrietta schooled her features into an expression of uninformative blandness, but after one good look at her face, Melinda glanced at her mother's—and knew.

Melinda's face fell. "Oh." Halting in front of her parents, she took her mother's hand, then looked at Henrietta. "It's not good news, is it?"

Henrietta grimaced. "It's not the news you wanted to hear."

Melinda glanced over her shoulder, but James had melted into the crowd and was no longer visible. Drawing in a breath, Melinda clutched her mother's hand more tightly and, head rising, faced Henrietta. "Tell me."

Mrs. Wentworth glanced meaningfully at the other guests. "This really might not be the best place to discuss this, dear."

Melinda frowned. "But I have to know. How can I face him again otherwise?"

"Perhaps," Mr. Wentworth suggested, "we might return home to discuss the matter in private." He looked at Henrietta. "If we could impose on Miss Cynster to oblige?"

Henrietta hadn't intended to leave the Montagues' house until later, but faced with three earnestly entreating expressions, she inclined her head. "Yes, of course. I have my parents' carriage. I'll follow you to Hill Street."

She trailed the Wentworths as they made their way to Lady Montague's side. While Melinda and Mrs. Wentworth thanked her ladyship for the evening's entertainment, Henrietta stood back and idly scanned the crowd. There were few present she did not know, few she couldn't immediately place in terms of family and connections.

She was absentmindedly surveying the heads when her gaze collided with James Glossup's.

Standing across the room, he was watching her intently.

The Wentworths took their leave and moved toward the door. Wrenching her gaze from James's, Henrietta smiled at Lady Montague and made her farewells, then followed the Wentworths.

She told herself not to look, but she couldn't resist glancing back.

James was still watching her, but his eyes had narrowed; the austere planes of his handsome face seemed harder, his expression almost harsh.

Henrietta met his gaze, held it for an instant,

then she turned and walked out of the ballroom.

On the other side of the room, James Glossup softly swore.

"*What* I've learned is that Mr. Glossup needs to marry in order to release additional funds from his grandaunt's estate." Ensconced in an armchair by the drawing room fire in the Wentworths' Hill Street house, Henrietta paused to sip the tea Mrs. Wentworth had insisted they all required.

Seated in the armchair opposite, with his daughter and wife on the chaise to his left, Mr. Wentworth frowned. "So he's not a fortune hunter after Mellie's dowry?"

Setting her cup on its saucer, Henrietta shook her head. "No—he has funds enough, but to release the balance of his grandaunt's fortune he has to marry. As I understand it, the old lady wanted to ensure that he did, so she made it a condition of her will."

Mr. Wentworth snorted. "I suppose that's one way an old lady can force a whelp to the altar, but not with my girl."

"No, indeed!" Mrs. Wentworth agreed, then, clearly recalling that it was Melinda's opinion that, in this instance, carried the real weight, turned to her daughter. "That is . . . Mellie?"

Cup and saucer held in her lap, Melinda had been staring into the fire. Now she blinked, glanced at her mother, then looked across at Henrietta. "He's not in love with me, is he?"

Henrietta adhered to the absolute truth. "That I can't say. All I can tell you is what I know." She held Melinda's gaze, then gently said, "You would be a much better judge of that than I."

Melinda stared back for several moments, then her lips firmed. She shook her head. "He likes me, but no—he doesn't love me." She paused and took a long sip of her until-then neglected tea. Lowering the cup, she went on, "Truth be told, that's why I asked you to learn what you could of him. I already suspected from the way he behaved that there was some motive other than love behind his approach . . ." Lips twisting, Melinda waved and looked away.

Henrietta drained her cup, then set it on the saucer and shifted forward to place both on the low table before the chaise. "I should go. There's nothing more I have to add, and you'll want to think things through." She rose.

Melinda set down her cup and saucer and rose, too, as did her parents. "I'll see you out."

"Thank you again for being such a good friend to Mellie." Mr. Wentworth gruffly patted Henrietta's hand.

Henrietta took her leave of the senior Wentworths and followed Melinda into the front hall. As soon as the butler shut the drawing room door, Henrietta murmured, low enough that only Melinda, just ahead of her, could hear, "I'm truly sorry to be the bearer of such tidings."

Halting, Melinda swung to face her. Meeting her eyes, Melinda smiled, albeit weakly. "I admit I was hoping to hear I'd misjudged him, but, truly, you've been a godsend. I *don't* want to marry a man who doesn't love me, and all your information has done is confirm what I already suspected, and for that I'm truly grateful. You've made my decision so much easier."

Clasping Henrietta's shoulders, Melinda touched cheeks, then drew back and continued, "So yes, I'll be glum for a day or two, but I'll come around soon enough—you'll see."

"I hope so." Henrietta smiled back.

"I know so." Melinda sounded more certain with every passing minute. "You've helped so many of us now, and I'm sure none of us know what we would have done without you. You've saved countless young ladies from disappointing marriages—quite honestly, you deserve an award."

Henrietta humphed. "Nonsense. I just have better-than-average sources of information." And, although in the present circumstances she wasn't about to mention it, she'd confirmed countless other matches as being soundly based on love.

She allowed the butler to settle her cloak about her shoulders, then he opened the front door.

Melinda accompanied her out onto the front step, and immediately shivered as a chill breeze whipped up the street.

Henrietta caught her hand and pressed it. "Go inside. You'll catch your death—and my carriage is right there." She nodded across the street to where her parents' second town carriage stood waiting by the curb.

"All right." Melinda squeezed back. "Take care. No doubt we'll meet again soon."

Henrietta smiled, waited until Melinda retreated and shut the door, then, still smiling to herself, reassured by Melinda's ready acceptance that she truly hadn't been in love with James, either, she started down the steps.

While she might have no faith in finding love herself, she was staunchly in favor of love-matches per se; to her mind, love was the one protection that guaranteed a lady a happy and contented married life—

A man barreled into her, moving at shocking speed. The collision sent her reeling.

"Oh!" She would have fallen, but the man

whirled and grasped her shoulders, holding her before him, steadying her.

From the corner of her eye, she glimpsed a silver-mounted cane grasped in one gloved hand, registered that the glove was exquisitely made, of soft, pliable leather. She blinked and glanced at the man's face, but he was wearing a cloak with the hood up; with the streetlights behind him, his face was shrouded in shadow.

All she could see was the tip of his chin. As she watched, it firmed.

"My apologies. I didn't see you." The man's voice was deep, the diction clipped, but cultured.

Catching her breath, she replied, "I didn't see you either."

He paused; she sensed he was studying her face, her eyes.

"Miss! Are you all right?"

She raised her head; the gentleman glanced over his shoulder. They both saw her groom dropping down to the street, intent on hurrying to her aid.

Even as she called out, "It's quite all right, Gibbs," the gentleman looked back at her, released her, brusquely nodded, then swung away and strode quickly on down the street, disappearing into the gathering fog.

Henrietta mentally shook her head, briskly

straightened her skirts and cloak, then crossed to where her groom stood waiting to hand her into the carriage.

The instant the door shut, she sighed and sank back against the leather seat. The carriage rocked into motion; Upper Brook Street was only minutes away.

Relaxing, expecting to feel the usual uplifting swell of satisfaction at another motivation-investigation successfully concluded, she instead found her mind unexpectedly focusing on something else entirely.

On the image of James Glossup standing in Lady Montague's ballroom, watching her intently. On his expression as he'd realized she was following his intended out of the room.

He was Simon's friend; he would know her reputation.

She wondered what he was thinking now.

An Excerpt from

THE LADY RISKS ALL

*L*ord Julian Roscoe Neville Delbraith, second son of the Duke of Ridgware, was a wastrel. Indeed, profligate beyond belief, he gave the term new meaning. Tall, dark-haired, and dangerously handsome, he prowled the ton with the lazy grace of a well-bred panther whose appetites were perennially sated, as, indeed, he ensured they were. He was considered by the gentlemen to be a capital sort, one with whom many wished to claim acquaintance, while the ladies appreciated his ineffable elegance, his expertise on the dance floor, his ready charm, and his occasionally exercised rapier wit. His attire, naturally, was invariably exquisite, and his horses turned Corinthians green. Wine, women, and gaming, in reverse order, were his principal occupations, which surprised no one; the Delbraiths had a long and venerable history of spawning males with an addiction to wagering. It ran in the blood.

That said, Lucasta, Lord Julian's mother, acknowledged Savior of the Delbraiths in the recent generation, was credited with having been sufficiently strong in her handling of Marcus, Julian's father, to have preserved the family fortunes. Marcus would have liked to have gambled his income away, but Lucasta had put her foot down and vetoed it. Adamantly. More, her firstborn son, George, was the first Delbraith in generations uncounted to have escaped the family curse.

Some felt that Lucasta's sterling efforts with Marcus and George had left her with insufficient reserves to effect a similar transformation with Julian, while others considered Julian's headstrong will beyond even his mother's ability to rein in, even had she been free to concentrate solely on him. In society's eyes, Julian was the epitome of the archetypal male Delbraith.

Yet to society and the family, Julian's enthusiastic embracing of the Delbraith curse mattered not at all. George was the heir.

Large, solid, quiet, and rather stuffily reserved, unlike his younger brother, George appeared to have no vices at all. While Julian could be counted on to be flippant, irreverent, and entertaining, George stood with his hands behind his back and said as little as he could. In short, George was boring, but that, too, wasn't a concern, because, after all, George was *safe*.

Consequently, when, on Marcus's death, George succeeded to the title, the family and society smiled. They continued to smile when George contracted an eminently suitable marriage with Caroline, daughter of the Earl of Kirkcombe, a sensible young lady well-regarded within the ton.

Caroline, following her mother-in-law's lead, considered George a paragon, at least with respect to his lack of susceptibility to the family curse. That she found him significantly less of a paragon in more private arenas she kept very much to herself; outwardly, she championed George at every turn, and society nodded approvingly. Unsurprisingly therefore, Caroline had no time for the rakishly attractive, outrageously dissolute Julian; her attitude made it clear that she regarded him as a potentially corrupting influence, one she wished to keep well distanced from her husband, herself, and the child she was soon carrying.

Not at all insensitive, Julian bowed to his sister-in-law's unspoken wishes; she, after all, was his brother's duchess. His visits to the family estate, Ridgware, in Staffordshire, previously quite frequent when he would dutifully call on his mother and then stay to play with his three much younger sisters, grew further apart, eventually dwindling to rare. The great house's staff, who saw far more than anyone supposed, counted that a real shame, but no one paid their opinion any heed.

Then Caroline's baby was born and proved to be a son. Christened Henry George Neville Delbraith, the boy bore all the physical hallmarks of a true Delbraith. Viewing said signs with due concern, Caroline swore that, come hell or high water, her son would never be touched by the Delbraith curse.

On the morning of the christening, Julian arrived at the church, sat with his mother and sisters, then under Caroline's baleful eye, feeling very much like the wicked witch of the fables, he passed his entirely innocuous christening gift to his mother to convey to his nephew, and immediately the service was concluded, shook his brother's hand, civilly wished his sister-in-law and the bundle held tightly—protectively—in her arms well, and drove himself back to London.

Subsequently, Julian only called on his mother and sisters when Caroline, and preferably baby Henry, too, were not—at least at that moment—under the same roof. If George was about, Julian would look in on him, but with such dissimilar characters and the weight of the title on George's shoulders, the brothers had never had all that much in common; a comment, a shared observation, and they parted, amicably, but distantly.

Meanwhile Julian filled his life with his customary round of gambling and dissipation; cards, dice, horse racing—anything racing—he was always willing to gauge the odds and sport his blunt accordingly. Dalliance, with Cyprians initially, but increasingly with bored matrons of his own class, filled whatever time he had to spare. His reputation as a wine connoisseur continued, but no one could recall ever seeing him in his cups. Then again, it was widely acknowledged that being three sheets to the wind while wagering large sums was never a winning proposition, and everyone knew Julian took his worship at the altar of his family's curse very seriously.

And the years rolled on.

Through those years, if any had requested enlightenment as to Lord Julian Delbraith's financial state from anyone in the ton, the answer would have been that Lord Julian was certain to be one step away from point-non-plus. From falling into the River Tick and very likely drowning. To all seasoned observers it was inconceivable that anyone could maintain such a profligate lifestyle, and wager so consistently and so extravagantly, without outrunning the constable. Gamblers always lost, if not immediately, then ultimately; everyone knew that.

Caroline, Duchess of Ridgware, certainly subscribed to that view. More, she believed her feckless brother-in-law was draining the family coffers, but whenever she attempted to raise the issue with her husband, George scowled and told her she was mistaken. When, driven by the need to protect her son's inheritance, she pressed, George's lips tightened and he coldly and categorically assured her that Julian received only the modest quarterly stipend due to him under their father's will and nothing more—that Julian had never requested further funds from the estate, not even from George personally. Caroline didn't believe it, but faced with her husband's uncharacteristic flash of temper she had to accept his word and retreat.

In actual fact, only two people knew the truth about Lord Julian's financial position—his gentlemen's gentleman, Rundle, and Jordan Draper, the son of the family's man of business. At Julian's request Jordan had assumed the handling of Julian's financial affairs, thus separating them from his brother's ducal holdings. Only those two knew that Julian was one of the Delbraiths who cropped up every third or so generation. He was one of the Delbraiths who won. He didn't win every bet, but over any period of time he always came out ahead. Not since he had, at the age of five, first discovered the joys of wagering had he ever ended a week a true loser; some weeks he only gained a farthing, but overall, he never, ever, lost money.

It fascinated Jordan Draper that no one had ever questioned why it was that a family as old as the Delbraiths, cursed with such a ruinous compulsion, had never run themselves or their estates into the ground. Through his association with Julian, Jordan knew the answer. Grandfather, father, son—over the three generations, one male at least would have the winning touch. Of course, that no longer mattered as, thanks to Lucasta and her influence on Marcus and subsequently George, the family was no longer hostage to the curse. The curse had been defeated . . . but in administering Julian's accounts and investments, Jordan had to wonder if, all in all, the family truly was better off.

Consequently, Julian's life, along with his extravagant lifestyle, rolled on largely uneventfully. He was well aware of the ton's view of him; the knowledge reinforced his natural cynicism and made him inwardly smile.

Until late one night in 1811, a knock fell on the street door of his lodgings in Duke Street.

It was November, and the weather had turned bleak. Few of the ton were still in town, which explained why Julian was sitting by his fire, his feet propped on a stool and an open book in one hand. At the knock, he'd raised his head; hearing Rundle's footsteps pass the parlor on the way to the front door, he waited, vaguely wondering—

"My lord!" Rundle burst into the room without knocking, not his usual practice. "It's Higginbotham from Ridgware."

Looking past Rundle at the senior groom from his brother's estate, taking in the man's disheveled appearance and grave face, Julian straightened. "My mother?"

Higginbotham blinked, then shook his head. "No, m'lord. It's your brother."

"George?" Julian couldn't imagine why George would have sent Higginbotham racing to town to summon him, the wastrel younger brother. "What's he want?"

Higginbotham looked like he'd swallowed his tongue, but then he shook his head again. "His Grace don't want anything. He put a pistol to his head and pulled the trigger. He's dead. We think you'd better come."

*J*ulian drove like the devil and reached Ridgware midmorning. Leaving his phaeton in the stable yard, he crossed to the house, entering via the side door. A pall had fallen over the mansion; the silence was oppressive. His footsteps echoed as he walked onto the tiles of the front hall. For a moment he stood silently, at a loss. Higginbotham had known nothing of what had driven George to such a rash and irreversible act. To an act so out of character.

To an act so *inexplicable.*

A sound down one corridor had Julian turning.

From the shadows, an older man in a fastidiously neat dark suit emerged. "Thank you for coming so promptly, my lord."

Lips tight, Julian nodded. "Draper." This was Draper senior, his brother's man of business, Jordan's father. The Draper offices were in Derby, much nearer than London. Julian searched Draper's face. "Do you have any idea why George . . . I still can't believe it . . . why he took his life?"

Sober and solemn, Draper nodded; he looked pale, worn down—significantly more aged than Julian remembered him. "Sadly, my lord, I do. That's why I was relieved the staff had taken it upon themselves to send for you. This is a bad business, and we'll need decisions made quickly if we're to protect the family."

"Protect . . . ?" Julian frowned. "I don't understand."

"I know." Draper waved down the corridor. "If you will come to the office, I'll endeavor to explain."

Julian hesitated. "My mother?"

"Prostrated by the shock, as is the duchess, but the doctor was here yesterday and both were sedated. I'm told they might wake in a few hours."

"My sisters? And Henry? Good God, the poor boy's the duke now."

"Indeed, but the staff have the young people well in hand, and I fear . . ." Draper broke off and rubbed his forehead. "I fear our discussion won't wait, my lord. In such a situation, time is of the essence."

Draper was a solid man, a steady, unruffleable, conscientious man, which was one reason Julian had chosen his son as his own man of affairs. Growing even more puzzled—more alarmed— Julian nodded. "Very well." He gestured. "Lead on."

Following Draper down the corridor, he asked, "When did it happen?"

"Yesterday morning, my lord. The staff heard the shot at eleven o'clock, I believe. They had to break down the library door, but of course there was nothing they could do."

Julian had had time to think during the long hours of the drive. "How many others know of George's death?"

"At the moment, my lord, I believe the knowledge is restricted to the indoor staff, the stable staff, and the family. And the doctor and myself, of course."

"So we have a chance of concealing the suicide." His first thought was for his sisters, his mother, for Henry, and even for his sister-in-law; a suicide in the family, whatever the reason, cast a long social shadow.

Draper hesitated before saying, "Possibly." He didn't sound at all certain.

Julian followed Draper into the estate office.

Draper waved him to the chair behind the desk. "It will make it easier for me to show you the accounts."

"Accounts?" Lowering himself into the chair, Julian frowned. "Why do I need to see the accounts?"

Lifting a heavy ledger from a shelf, Draper turned and met his gaze. "I regret to inform you, my lord, that your brother wasn't, as was generally supposed, immune to the Delbraith curse."

"*Hell's bells!*" Julian speared the fingers of both hands through his hair and stared at the evidence of George's addiction. In the past half hour, Draper had laid ledger after ledger before him, driving home one very simple fact.

George had succeeded where all Delbraiths before him had failed. He'd run the estate into the ground, then had compounded the damage by mortgaging every last asset to the hilt.

Lowering his hands, Julian sat back. "All right." His mind was whirling, juggling figures and sums, chances and possibilities. He now understood why Draper had wanted him there. "Tot up the sum. All of it. And send for Jordan—tell him to bring all my current accounts."

"Yes, my lord." Draper hesitated, then admitted, "I took it upon myself to send for Jordan earlier—he should arrive within the hour."

Julian raised his gaze to the older man's face. "That was strangely presumptuous of you." He said it without heat, more as a question.

Draper met his gaze. "I apologize, my lord, but I've known you and your brother since you were infants. I knew the family could count on your help, and, as I've said, we—"

"Don't have time." Julian grimaced, then

nodded curtly. "Very well." He pushed back his chair. "I'm going up to see my sisters. Send for me when Jordan arrives."

*H*e found Millicent, Cassandra, and Edwina in the small upstairs parlor they used as their own. They'd been informed that George had died, but they had been told nothing else. However, having heard the shot and witnessed the resulting furor, they were more than capable of putting two and two together.

"He killed himself, didn't he?" Millicent, fourteen years old and bidding fair to becoming another Lucasta, sat sideways along the window seat, knees to her chest, and cut straight to the heart of the matter.

Having exchanged kisses and longer-and-tighter-than-usual hugs with all three, Julian sat on the cushion beyond Millicent's toes and hesitated, wondering what he could spare them, whether he should . . .

Cassie, eleven, snorted. "Just *tell* us—you know we'll get it out of the staff if you don't."

Julian sighed and complied, keeping an eye on Edwina, just ten, to make sure nothing he said was too much of a shock.

"But . . . why?" Millicent frowned. "It's a thoroughly horrible thing to do—he must have had a reason."

This was the tricky part. "I understand from Draper that George had begun gambling. It seems the curse had caught up with him, and rather than risk the estate and his family, George . . . well, he put a stop to it."

Julian hoped they would swallow the white lie.

All three frowned, considering, then Cassie humphed. "That sounds like George. So stuffy that he couldn't bear asking you for help." Cassie turned her gray eyes on Julian. "You've been living with the curse all your life and it's never hurt you—and you've never hurt the estate or the family, either."

He managed a weak smile. "Sadly, George wasn't me."

"No." Millie swung her legs down and briefly clasped his arm. "You're made of much sterner stuff. But what about the taint? Of suicide, I mean?"

"You don't need to worry about that. The doctor left a note saying that in the circumstances he would suggest we put it about that George died suddenly and unexpectedly of apoplexy."

The three thought for a moment, then Edwina said, "Well, then, I suppose what we need to do next is get some mourning clothes so we can see George off in proper style."

Millie grimaced. "True. He might have been an idiot, but he was our noble idiot and he sacrificed himself for us, so we should at least do him proud in the matter of his funeral."

From the corner of his eye, Julian spotted a gig, driven by Jordan Draper, come bowling up the drive.

"We should go and talk to Mama," Cassie said. "Discussing clothes might cheer her up, or at least take her mind off the manner of George's passing." She looked at Julian. "Have you seen her yet?"

"No. Not yet." He paused, then said, "Why don't you three go and distract her, and tell her I'm here, and that I'll be up to speak with her as soon as I can?" He rose along with the girls. "I have to go and sort things out with Draper, just to get everything squared away. Tell Mama I'll come up as soon as I've finished."

His sisters nodded and hugged him again, then they all quit the parlor. Parting from the girls in the corridor, Julian surreptitiously sighed with relief; that had gone better than he'd hoped.

*H*e spent the next hours with the Drapers, father and son, then they were joined by Minchinbury, the family solicitor. The office was crowded with all four of them in it, but no one suggested they take their discussions into a less secure and well-shielded room.

Minchinbury confirmed that George's will named Julian as sole executor, and also joint guardian of three-year-old Henry. In regard to the latter, Julian merely nodded and set that problem aside for later; one hellish scenario at a time.

"There's no way around it," Jordan eventually concluded. "No matter how we structure payments, even if we liquidate every saleable unentailed asset and devote the entirety of the estate income to said payments, the outgoings still far exceed the duke's ability to pay."

While they'd been going over the horrendous figures, a plan had taken shape in Julian's mind. It was beyond outrageous, but outrageous was something he did well. Across the desk, he met Jordan's eyes. "Factor in my funds—all of them. Liquidate my assets, all of them, and add them in, too—reduce the capital owed. Leave me . . ." He considered, then said, "Ten thousand in cash. Assume an ongoing income through me of . . ."

That took a little longer to calculate, but eventually he named a sum.

Draper and Minchinbury looked startled, but Jordan only grimaced, jotted down the figures, and started reworking the complex web of mortgage and loan repayments again.

While he did, Draper and Minchinbury traded looks . . . and slowly worked out Julian's direction. It was Minchinbury who, faintly shocked, finally looked at Julian. "My lord . . . what are you planning?"

Julian held up a finger and patiently waited while Jordan did his sums.

Eventually, Jordan blew out a breath. "We're close. Just a whisker in it." He looked at Julian. "You could pull it off."

Julian hadn't needed to explain to Jordan what he was thinking of doing; Jordan had worked for him for long enough to guess what he might, and could, do, but he was grateful for the younger man's unequivocal support. "You've included the running of this house and the estate in general, the usual payments to my mother, the girls, and the duchess, and left the girls' portions intact?"

"Well, the girls' portions are already long gone," Jordan said, "but that will return them to their previous amounts by the time each of them reach sixteen. I've also included an escalating amount for Henry in the years to come, starting from his fifth birthday."

"Good man." Julian paused to gather his arguments, then transferred his gaze to Draper and Minchinbury. "What I'm proposing to do, gentlemen, is this."

He told them his plan, the whole of it; if he was to succeed in saving the Delbraiths—family, title, and estate—he needed them on his side. At first, they were shocked, then aghast as the full ramifications of what he was proposing came clear in their minds, but finally, like Jordan, they, too, accepted that, when it came to it, he had no other choice.

George had taken the easy way out and left Julian to rescue the Delbraiths.

$\mathcal{H}$is interview with his mother was difficult, not least because Lucasta was inclined to blame herself for George's disgrace.

Seated in an armchair angled before the wide window in her sitting room, a still handsome woman with graying hair pulled back from a grief-stricken face, she clenched a damp handkerchief in one fist. "I should have seen it! I can't *believe* I missed the signs."

Contrary to general assumptions, Julian got along well with his mother; they were much alike when it came to will. They'd long ago reached an accommodation; Lucasta didn't try to push him, and he didn't push back.

Standing gazing out over the rolling lawns to the trees of the home wood, he sighed. "Mama, if *I* didn't see anything, there wasn't anything to be seen. He was . . . excellent at hiding it."

"He deceived us. He *betrayed* us." After a moment, in a quieter voice, Lucasta asked, "For how long?"

Julian hesitated, but he knew better than to try to lie to her. Turning, he said, "According to Draper, since he started at Eton, but initially the amounts were small enough not to alert Papa or you. Only after he inherited did he start wagering larger sums."

Helplessly, Lucasta shook her head. "You never heard any whisper?"

"No." Which said a great deal about what establishments George had frequented. Any socially accepted hell, and Julian would have heard of it, so George had slid into the underworld to sate his addiction.

Slowly, Lucasta drew in a deep breath, then exhaled and raised her chin. "What's done is done. We'll do as Doctor Melrose suggested—George died of an apoplexy. We'll bury him with all due circumstance. And then"—she looked at Julian— "we'll pick up the pieces and rebuild." She paused, eyes narrowing on him. "So." She heaved a tight sigh. "Given George blew out his brains rather than face the consequences, tell me—how bad is it?"

He didn't try to soften the news—pointless where she was concerned. His mother had always been fierce in defense of her family; she would detect any prevarication and, terrier-like, drag the truth from him. So he drew up another armchair, sat and told her all, and when the shock, unsurprisingly, held her stunned and silent, he smoothly continued, "I've spoken with the Drapers, both of them, and with Minchinbury, and worked out a plan. It's desperate, but for us these are desperate times. They've agreed that it's our only possible way forward—we've canvassed every other course, and none will get us through this except what I propose."

She looked him in the eye. "I'm not going to like your plan, am I?"

"No, but it is the only plan we have." He proceeded to tell her the whole of it.

She heard him out in silence.

Then they argued.

That he'd expected; he held to his guns and

eventually, bit by bit, inch by inch, she backed down.

Except, to his surprise, over one aspect, and on that she wouldn't budge, wouldn't shift, would not concede.

"I have lost one son—I will not lose you, too. *No!*" She held up a hand. "I appreciate that to be successful your plan makes open association impossible, *but*"—she fixed her eyes on his—"you will continue to visit this house, to visit me and your sisters. They are my daughters and are as capable of keeping your secrets as I am. You will *not* cut yourself off from us—and I assure you we will not let you go." Her eyes filled. "That, my dear, is something you cannot ask of us. If your plan is to succeed, you will need to factor that in."

He hadn't expected such a vehement reaction. Searching her face, knowing her adamantine will, he reconsidered, then nodded. "Very well. But my visits will be, for want of a better word, furtive."

"Secret." She nodded. "You know the staff will do anything for you, so that won't be a problem."

"The girls . . ." He grimaced. "I'll leave it to you to tell them—you'll know better than I how to put it, and I don't have time for the inevitable arguments and explanations. Jordan and I must leave for London as soon as possible. If we're to paper over the gaping holes George has left in the family's financial façade, we need to act immediately."

Lucasta's eyes searched his face, then she quietly asked, "And Caroline? I'll explain to her if you wish."

Lips thinning, he shook his head. "No—I'll speak with her. She's Henry's other guardian. She and I are going to have to find a way to work together, for Henry's sake if nothing else."

He rose.

Lucasta rose, too, gripped his arm, and stretched up to plant a kiss on his cheek. "Go, my dear. I know you must."

She released him and turned away, but not before he saw a tear slide down her cheek.

His interview with his sister-in-law set the seal on a long and horrendous day.

As he approached her suite, he saw Draper and Minchinbury emerge from Caroline's sitting room. They closed the door behind them and came along the gallery. When he and the pair met, they all halted.

Minchinbury spoke. "I've explained the terms of the will to the duchess. She understands that you are sole executor and also her son's co-guardian, and comprehends the rights that are yours by virtue of those facts."

Julian felt his lips twist. "And how did she take that news?"

Minchinbury grimaced. "Not well, but she had to be told. At least she now knows and understands the situation."

"We also informed her of the financial straits the late duke left behind." Draper's lips primmed. "I explained that, contrary to her long-held belief, you have never drained any undue resources from the estate, and that the current situation has arisen entirely through the late duke's depredations. We did not, of course, venture to explain your plan, although we did allude to the fact that you had one, and that, given the situation, we believe it is the only route by which the family, and indeed the dukedom, can be saved from financial devastation."

Julian looked from one to the other. "Let me see if I understand this correctly—you've left the duchess knowing that whatever I propose, she must agree if she wishes to save herself and her son from ruin?"

Both men thought, then both nodded. "We"—Minchinbury flicked a glance at Draper—"have been privy to the duchess's view of you, my lord, and considered it our duty to clarify matters for Her Grace so that your words should fall on more fertile soil."

Draper nodded. "Least we could do to assist you with your plan."

Julian inclined his head. "Thank you, gentlemen. I appreciate your assistance."

Both bowed and stepped back. Minchinbury said, "If you need any assistance subsequently, my lord, please know you have only to ask."

Julian nodded and continued along the corridor. Reaching Caroline's sitting room, he didn't pause to let himself think but tapped on the door. Hearing a muffled "Come," he turned the knob and entered.

Caroline was standing with her back to the window, her arms wrapped tightly about her. Inclining his head, Julian closed the door, then walked toward her. "My condolences. I would it were otherwise, but we have to talk." Halting a yard away, he met her blue eyes. "Minchinbury and Draper told me they'd explained the situation. Is there anything about it you don't understand?" He kept his tone even, uninflected and distantly polite.

Her face stripped of all masks, Caroline stared up at him; he could see the emotions, the questions, the rage, roiling behind her eyes. In the end, she rasped out one word, hoarse and ragged. "*Why*?"

Julian shook his head. "He couldn't help himself."

"But—" She broke off, then waved a hand and looked away. "I can't . . ." She hauled in a breath and, lifting her head, continued without looking at him. "I'm still finding it hard to . . . accept that, for all these years, while I've been imagining you the villain, it was him all along."

Julian frowned. "You suspected?"

"Not him." She laughed harshly. "Never him. But some of my jewelry—it's paste, not real. Even some of what used to be real is now paste." She glanced at Julian. "I thought he'd used the jewels to pay your debts, perhaps thinking that I would never notice the difference in the stones, and that in his mind that was better than drawing from the estate—" Her breath hitched and she swung away. "Oh, you needn't tell me—I can't believe how stupid I've been."

He didn't have time for hysterics, even of this sort. "Caroline—if I'm to avert financial catastrophe, I need to act quickly."

She cast him a bitter glance. "According to Minchinbury and Draper, I have no choice but to allow you to do whatever you wish, not if I want to continue to live here in comfort with Henry, or for my son to have any kind of future at all."

This was the downside of the older men's well-intentioned interference. "In that, they're correct, but what they didn't make clear was that for my plan to succeed, you, too, need to play a part. And for that, you need to know what the plan is."

Caroline considered him for a long moment, then settled on her feet facing him, arms tightly folded, and nodded. "All right. Tell me your plan."

She didn't sit, much less invite him to. So he stood and told her his plan.

When he'd finished, she stared all but open-mouthed at him.

After a minute ticked by, he baldly asked, "Well? Will you do your part? Play the role you obviously have to play to carry the fiction off?"

She blinked, stared again. "I . . . don't understand."

His temper was getting the better of him. "It's a simple enough question. Will you—"

"No, not that. I . . ." She lowered her arms and drew a huge breath. She paused for a second, then, her gaze on his face, said, "You're proposing to sacrifice yourself. *Why*? That's what I don't understand—what I don't trust. If I accept this plan of yours and actively support it, I'll be placing myself, and even more my son and his future, in utterly insurmountable debt to you."

He thought, then nodded. "True."

She laughed, a broken, discordant sound, and turned away.

"Caroline." By main force, he kept his tone even, calm. "Are you really proposing to let your pride dictate your actions even now, and to reject my help?"

She glanced at him, met his eyes.

A distant, high-pitched shriek reached him—a sound of happiness, not despair. Glancing through the window, he saw his sisters and Henry come out of the wood. They'd been for a walk and were returning, Millie and Cassie swinging a delighted Henry between them. He was only three; the reality of his father's death hadn't yet touched him. Two footmen and a nursemaid followed behind, talking quietly while they watched over the foursome.

Julian looked at Caroline. He was much taller; she couldn't see what he could.

Although tempted to grasp her arm and haul her across, he beckoned to her and stepped closer to the window. "You want to know why I'm doing this?" When she joined him, he pointed at the group below. "That's why. None of the four down there—hell, none of the seven—have done anything to deserve the future they will have if I don't act to fix this. And there is only one way."

He watched her watching her son and let that sink in.

After a moment, she moistened her lips and more quietly asked, "No other way?"

He hesitated, then said, "The Delbraith curse got the family into this. It's only right that the Delbraith curse get us out of it again."

"But at what cost?"

"Regardless of the cost. And, ultimately, that's my decision to make, not yours."

She continued watching for a moment more, then her features firmed and she nodded. "All right. I agree. I'll do whatever I have to to . . . shore up the situation."

One hurdle down. He drew breath, metaphorically girded his loins, and approached the next, the even higher and more thorny one. "Speaking of the curse, I have one stipulation which is entirely nonnegotiable. In return for acting as I must to save the family—yourself and Henry included—you will ensure that Henry knows the truth about his father's death, that it's never hidden from him."

"*What*?" Caroline swung to face him. "You can't be serious! He's a baby—"

"Not now, obviously. I mean as soon as he's old enough to know—to ask. Because he will. I don't want you hiding the curse from him." He held her gaze. "I'm not doing what I'm about to do only to have you encourage him to think he's immune to the curse and so throw everything away the instant he reaches his majority." She opened her mouth. Julian pointed a finger at her nose and spoke first. "What's more, when I come to visit, as his guardian I'll expect to meet him, to talk with him. You can be present if you wish, but I will speak with him."

Caroline's face set. "No. I won't have you—"

"Caroline." The steel in his voice cut her off. He held her gaze and ruthlessly stated, "Neither you nor Mama saw the curse in George. Try to 'protect' Henry, and you'll make the same mistake Mama made with George. The curse will still bite, but he'll hide it. If he does, you won't see it. I will because I know what to look for—and I assure you that with Henry, I'll be watching." He searched her eyes. "Understand this—the curse is real. It's an inherited disease—if Henry gets help, the right help, it can be managed. Pretend it's not there and it will eat him alive, just as it did George."

"And what about you?" Caroline produced a credible sneer. "Is your addiction so well managed then?"

He was silent for a moment, then said, "As things stand, my addiction is what's going to stand between you and Henry and the poorhouse. Think about that before you dismiss my use of it. Also as things stand, I'm the only one living who has personal experience of the curse—who knows what Henry will face as he grows, who knows the tricks of dealing with the compulsion." He paused for a moment, his eyes locked with hers, then more quietly said, "I know this is hard for you to accept, but as matters stand, I am Henry's only hope for a future, both financially and personally."

Until he'd said the words, he hadn't realized how true they were—how much responsibility he was taking on.

Not that it mattered; in this he had no choice.

When Caroline said nothing, simply chewed her lower lip and looked shaken and lost, he stepped back and turned to the door. With his hand on the knob, he paused, then glanced back at her. "Don't risk your son, Caroline—if you want to keep him safe, you'll do exactly as I've said."

She swung to face the window and didn't reply.

Julian opened the door and left.

Half an hour later, having bid good-bye to his sisters and his small nephew, Julian tooled his phaeton down the long drive, then whipped up his horses and headed for London.

In the small hours of the morning, he drew

rein outside the stables near his lodgings. Handing over the ribbons to a sleepy stable lad, Julian walked slowly out into the street.

Sinking his hands into his greatcoat pockets, through the quiet darkness, he strolled toward Duke Street, and finally allowed himself to think of what he was about to do, something he'd refused to dwell on during the long journey; the activity smacked too much of a dying man's last thoughts.

Reaching his lodgings, he climbed the steps, put his key to the lock, and opened the door.

Stepping inside, he shut the door.

And his life as Lord Julian Delbraith was, quite simply, no more.

The Treaty of the Kingdoms of Fire & Ice,

Or,

The Imposter Bride

GAELEN FOLEY

$\mathcal{P}$rince Tor of Rydalburg threw down his sword, chest heaving, his face streaked with dried blood and black powder. The din of battle still rang in his ears. The smell of cannon fire clung to his sweat-drenched uniform, and his shoulder ached from wielding the weapon for countless hours. But he had fulfilled his task. Another war won.

"What are you waiting for? Call the attack!" cried King Hakon. "Don't just stand there. Finish them!"

"They are finished, Father. What more do you want me to do? I've already cut off their general's bloody leg. Trust me. I know this foe. They are defeated," he said wearily. "They just need a moment to let that fact sink in." He couldn't even remember the cause of this particular episode of

the long-standing conflict between the neighbor-
ing kingdoms of Rydalburg and Saardova.

But his father was, predictably, unsatisfied. The
older man, slightly shorter and much stouter than
he, sent Tor a glare, then marched over to the artil-
lery captain and pointed past the groaning southern army spread out across the plain below them.
"Aim for the city," he instructed. "I want nothing
left of their capital but rubble—"

"Belay that order," Tor clipped out sharply.

His father turned to him in shock. "What did
you say?"

"There is no need for this. There are women
and children in that city, Father."

"You lack the killer instinct of your ancestors,
son. Let me show you how it's done."

"Sire, hear me out! Saving face is everything
to the Saardovans. If we humiliate them with de-
struction of their city on top of defeat, they will
opt for a proud but senseless death over surrender." Then he snorted. "They likely would've quit
all this by now if it weren't for their stupid hothead, Prince Orsino."

"So?" His father scoffed. "Let them fight. We
will pound them into dust. Now, give the order to
the gun-crews."

"I will not, sir."

"How dare you defy me?" His father stepped

closer, fixing him with a pugnacious glare despite the fact that he was half a foot shorter than Tor. "I gave you an order! I am your father and your King!"

"And I am your successor, and when you're dead, I would like there to be something left for me to rule. Besides," he added calmly, "why would I break a vase I'm about to own?"

"What?" Hakon furrowed his brow, turning as Tor moved past him to gaze out across the bloodied plain.

"Be happy, Sire," he murmured. "I'm about to double the size of our holdings."

"How do you intend to do that?"

"By marrying the Princess of Saardova." He beckoned for the messenger, then put together a small contingent to ride out for a parley. "The price of my mercy."

*A*ll that had been three months ago, and now, here they were, on the morning the wedding caravan was to set out from the lush, exotic capital of sensual Saardova, a place full of mystery and whimsy, kissed by ocean breezes.

So he'd heard. His bride was expected to arrive by tonight. Tor wanted the marriage treaty sealed up by tomorrow. Not the most romantic way of looking at his pending nuptials, perhaps, but then, unseemly emotionalism was the domain of the Saardovans.

Sentimentality was promptly beaten out of young Rydalburg children before they reached puberty. They were a warrior people of Viking origin, long since settled in their little corner of the Alps. Disciplined, hard, matter-of-fact. This practical nature had allowed King Hakon to come around to Tor's plan once the old chieftain's rage had puttered out.

He still fumed a little now and then about it. "A mistress, yes, but I can't believe you're willing to marry some sleazy southern belly dancer."

"Now, Sire, that is no way to speak about my future wife. They say the Princess Giulietta is a great beauty."

And a great pain in the arse, Tor admitted to himself, but he did not say it aloud.

No need to bait his father.

Besides, he was not surprised in the least by what his spies had reported. All Saardovans were famously temperamental, as fiery as they liked their food. With her royal blood, Princess Giulietta had apparently got a larger-than-usual dose of lowland spice in her nature. She was rumored to be notoriously difficult, manageable only by her chief lady-in-waiting, Minerva de Messina, the daughter of the very general whose leg he had cut off in the heat of battle.

Tor winced slightly. No doubt he had made a sworn enemy of this young woman, who was universally respected in her city as a model of womanly dignity and virtue. Or at least, what passed for virtue among that race of seducers.

He had been weighing the possible cost in girlish tantrums that he might pay if he forbade Giulietta from bringing her best friend to Rydalburg, but then his spies had told him there was no need for concern.

Lady Minerva would not be accompanying the princess to her new home. Oddly enough, she had been accepted as the first female ever allowed to enroll in the University of Saardova. Tor shrugged off this bizarre notion.

All that mattered to him was that the lady scholar was staying behind. He did not need a sworn enemy in the palace undermining him with his new bride.

Rumor had it that Lady Minerva was the only one who could keep a rein on the rebellious princess, her junior by a couple of years, but no matter. Giulietta would quickly learn how to behave herself properly once she got here.

His sister, Princess Katarina, a maiden as pure as the winter snows, would help to make a lady of her. Tor himself was also prepared to be a good, calm influence on his spoiled Saardovan bride, for nothing ever really moved him.

His own nature was cool and controlled. Let her rail away; tears; yelling; it did not signify. She might come to hate him. In fact, from what he heard, she already did. But he did not particularly care.

What mattered was that the war was over. He had expanded his territory and ended the strain it put on his people. As for this marriage, why, it was only a tool of political expediency.

No doubt it was not what Giulietta's girlish heart and overemotional southern nature would have hoped for, but too bad. All that unseemly romantic rot was the purview of slimy Saardovans like her brother, Prince Orsino.

Falling in love? Rydalburg warriors like Tor scoffed at the notion.

It was as absurd as a female attending university.

I know, daughter, this was not what you had envisioned for your life. But the House of Messina will always do its duty."

"Yes, Papa," Minerva quietly agreed.

Her father laid his hands tenderly on her shoulders and gazed down into her soulful brown eyes.

General Farouk de Messina, commander of Saardova's beaten army, had lost a leg to Rydalburg along with the battle. But the keenest loss of all was at hand. They both knew disaster was the likely result if she did not go with her flighty royal friend.

A rare tear glistened in the general's one good eye. (The other was covered by the eye patch.) "Defeat is bitter enough without also having to say farewell to my little girl," he said abruptly, lurching forward on his peg leg to embrace her.

Minerva hugged him back, squeezing her eyes shut against her tears. "All will be well, Papa," she tried to comfort him, knowing how much he blamed himself for everything. "No one could have led our forces better against those barbarians. We were outnumbered, and besides, they had the high ground. Wave after wave of those terrible cavalry charges . . ." She shuddered. "What infantry could withstand them? But at least now our people will have peace."

"As long as Her Highness can bear to do her duty."

Pulling back, Minerva smiled fondly at the old, sun-weathered soldier. "Don't worry, Papa. If

I have to drag Giulietta up to the altar myself, I will not let anything disrupt your treaty with the Horse Danes. Not even the tantrums of the most spoiled princess in the Mediterranean," she added in a confidential whisper.

"Go. Before I refuse to part with you."

"I love you, Papa."

"And I you." With tears in his eyes, he kissed her on the forehead then released her and sent her on her way.

Minerva drew her silken scarlet veil across the lower half of her face and headed for the door.

She paused in the doorway, however, glancing back uncertainly. For a moment, facing the prospect of being an exile, forced to dwell in enemy territory far from home, she feared her heart might break.

"What is it?" her father asked. "Did you forget to pack something?"

"Oh, Papa," she whispered, fairly quivering with her hidden rage. "How am I to stomach being in the same room with the man who did this to you?" she burst out. "It's bad enough poor, silly Giulietta has to marry this barbarian, but after what he did to you—"

"Now, now," he chided, glancing down ruefully at the sturdy wooden peg below his left knee. "It was a fair blow, and neatly executed."

"Papa! What a dense, perfectly male thing to say. You could have died!"

He gave her a hard look. "Prince Tor had the chance to kill me when I was on the ground; he did not. Remember that."

She let out a disgruntled sigh.

"None of us likes the terms of his treaty, Minerva, but if King Hakon had had his way, trust me, it would have been much worse. Because of the prince, we finally have a chance at lasting peace. Provided Her Highness doesn't ruin it for the rest of us."

"I won't let her," Minerva grumbled. "That's the only reason I'm doing this."

"I know," he answered softly, pride shining in his leathery face. "Farewell, my dear. Now go."

Minerva tore her gaze away from him and obeyed him, going out to where the royal guards waited to escort her back to Giulietta and the palazzo.

As she climbed down into the waiting gondola, she looked her last upon the sunny villa and committed it to memory: the brightly colored tiles of the fountain lilting in the central courtyard; the shady grape arbor where she had spent endless hours studying her books; the mounds of bright bougainvillea burgeoning against the white-washed walls; and the swaying palm trees peeking above the red-tiled roof.

As the royal guards poled her gondola through the lazy waters of the canal, she imprinted the sights of buildings and bridges on her mind, saying a particularly woeful farewell in her heart to the great University as they floated past. She was to have begun her classes in the autumn, but it seemed her country needed her to serve another role. She hung her head with a pang.

But if Papa was willing to give up a leg and an eye for Saardova, this was the least that she could do.

When her gondola drifted up to the restricted landing behind the royal palazzo, she found the entire wedding caravan gathered there. Everyone who would be traveling to Rydalburg had assembled. The camels were laden with luggage. The royal guards' Arabian horses pranced in place and tossed their long manes, as if the morning air made them eager to be under way. At least today they wouldn't be charging into a battle, she thought wryly.

Near the brightly adorned royal elephant she saw Giulietta surrounded by ambassadors and dignitaries, her royal mother weeping by her side.

Minerva braced herself to join the fray.

But then, a familiar face emerged from the crowd: Crown Prince Orsino, Giulietta's elder brother, abandoned the throng of well-wishers and came to hand Minerva up from her boat.

Black-haired and fiery-eyed, the Prince of Saardova was the object of countless ladies' dreams, but privately, Minerva found him a bit of a headache with his touchy pride, his moods—and his wandering hands.

Saardovan men were known for their passionate nature, which was probably half the reason they went to war with their northern neighbors once a decade.

Certainly it was why they insisted on taking several wives—at least the nobles. They had, they claimed, needs too powerful for any one woman to satisfy.

To Minerva, this backward and degrading practice, this excuse for lewd selfishness, was the reason she had privately made up her mind not to marry. One wife, one husband was quite sufficient.

At least the Rydalburgers had that much right.

Perhaps it was just as well that she was moving away, she thought as Orsino steadied her on solid ground. She suspected that the prince had it in the back of his mind to propose to her one day, and if he did, she did not see how she could get out of it.

He flashed a white-toothed smile. "My lady Minerva." He kissed her hand before escorting her toward his sister. "It's not going to be the same around here with you girls gone," he said with a sigh. "Who will I get to tease?"

"Oh, I'm sure you will find someone," she said wryly.

He stopped and turned to her with the morning sunlight dancing in his black, tousled curls. "You will look after her, won't you? I know I've always been a beastly brother, but I do care about my little sister."

"Of course, Your Highness," she said fondly in spite of herself.

His gaze caressed her. "You put my mind at ease," he replied in his effortlessly beguiling tone. "We all feel better knowing the brat will have you with her. Voice of reason whispering in her ear."

"Are you sure you won't come to the wedding, Your Highness?" she asked, changing the subject. "It would mean so much to your sister—"

"No." He held up his hand and looked away with a blaze of anger registering in his midnight eyes. "I cannot. Do not ask it of me. If this alliance spares our people, then so be it. But you must excuse me if I cannot bear to stand by and watch my baby sister married off to my mortal enemy."

"I understand. Be well, Your Highness." She

curtsied and took leave of the prince, rejoining her royal mistress.

The eighteen-year-old Giulietta finished her tearful goodbyes to her parents and her brother, then she and Minerva and the other ladies-in-waiting climbed up the dainty little ladder into the howdah perched atop the royal elephant's back.

With that, the wedding caravan set out: camels, wagons, horses, all. Gaily festooned as they all were, Giulietta held back her tears as they rode through the streets of Saardova.

She waved gracefully and with great drama to her people. The citizens, half cheering, half weeping for her, threw flower petals in the air and thanked her for how she was about to sacrifice herself to the barbarian prince.

In the distance Minerva could see the cobalt waters of the Mediterranean, the white sails of colorful fishing boats and the mighty war vessels that had done her homeland no good whatsoever against an inland foe.

Ah, well.

They rode in silence for some time after they had cleared the city and set out across the plain that had been the battlefield. It was quiet now, but grave markers here and there studded the fields where the fallen from both sides had been buried.

The princess leaned on the edge of the howdah and gazed off into the distance. "It's so unfair. I'll never again stand out on my balcony and watch the sunset gild the waves and turn the gardens pink." She turned to Minerva, pouting as only a princess could pout. "Why would he not come to Saardova?"

She shrugged. "He can do whatever he wants. He won. We lost."

"And I am to be the virgin sacrifice to the barbarian for this treaty's sake?" she asked bitterly, gazing homeward again. "Doesn't anyone care what I want?"

"They say he is handsome."

"Big, blond, blue-eyed. Aren't they all? I can't even tell them apart. He doesn't have a soul. None of them do. None of them have any feelings!"

"Come now, dearest. Our views of them are probably as inaccurate as their beliefs about us. This is a chance for both sides to learn the truth about each other. You'll be starting a whole new chapter in Saardovan history."

"Pfft," she said.

Minerva laughed. The other ladies-in-waiting smiled uneasily, slowly getting over their fear as she made light of it.

"Try to think of it as an adventure," she said for all their sakes. "And don't forget, Your Highness, those mountains over which you will be queen are packed with jewels."

Giulietta sent her a sideways smile. "You always know just what to say to me."

Soon the road climbed from the fertile lowlands of Saardova toward the mountain kingdom of their enemies. Great peaks loomed in the distance; around them, the colors changed from vibrant summer jewel tones to the dreamy watercolors seen in spring. Likewise, the temperature dropped by several degrees, and the ladies began to shiver in their delicate, flowing silks.

At the border, they were met by an elite contingent of Horse Danes, sent to escort them the rest of the way to Rydalburg. The Horse Dane cavalry officers wore smartly tailored indigo uniforms with gold epaulets and shiny gold buttons down their chests, red plumes on their gleaming helmets. They rode in perfect, precise formation—and Giulietta was right. None of their square, pale faces showed the slightest degree of emotion. They informed the wedding caravan that the journey was but three more hours.

Right on schedule (the northerners were always prompt, she'd heard), the caravan approached the walled castle-town of Rydalburg.

The ladies stared in openmouthed amazement at the white castle with its tall, fairy-tale spires.

The prince's home was nothing like the sumptuous palazzos of the lowlands, full of striped-marble columns and ogee-windows.

Its soaring lines and steep angles took Minerva's breath away, the turrets like the tips of lances thrusting at the pale Alpine sky.

They were received right away upon their arrival. The Saardovan ambassador hurried ahead of the princess and her retinue to announce Her Royal Highness to Their Majesties.

Arrayed across the dais at the far end of the great hall, waiting for them, stood the royal family of Rydalburg. King Hakon and Queen Ingmar greeted them. Princess Katarina curtsied.

Giulietta curtsied back. The two princesses looked about the same age, but were opposites in appearance. Not much could be seen of her behind her veil, but Minerva knew Giulietta's complexion was tanned, her brown hair filled with golden streaks from the sun; her dark, thick eyebrows expressed every shade of emotion she felt.

Princess Katarina's emotions were concealed behind a serene smile on her lips and the perfect curtain wall behind her pale blue eyes. Minerva sensed the steel in her and knew at once this girl was a great deal stronger than her delicate appearance would suggest. Katarina had the porcelain complexion of all the northern ladies; her silvery-blond hair was pulled back in a sleek bun like her mother's. Both women wore high-necked, long-sleeved gowns of somber, dark-toned velvet. Minerva was rather awed by their air of dignity.

But as hard as she was trying not to look at him, inevitably, her gaze wandered over to the fourth member of the royal family present: the Crown Prince, Tor of Rydalburg.

Her heart beat a trifle faster as she tried to assess him with a purely scientific eye. The broad-shouldered specimen stood well over six feet tall, towering over mere mortals like some rugged mountain rock formation. What on earth were they feeding these northern brutes to make them grow so strong and tall?

He had long golden hair that flowed back from his hard, square face like a lion's mane. His eyes were an interesting shade of stormy blue, but much too serious, of course. His nose was too big, his jawline too hard.

But his lips, well, she supposed she could find no flaw with his lips. They were nicely sculpted enough to cause an alarming stir in her spicy Saardovan blood.

Minerva tamped down the ridiculous reaction with an inward hiss at herself.

For one thing, he was about to marry her best friend. For another, he had cut off her father's leg.

And for a third, he had ruined her plans for an education, thanks to the bullying demands in his treaty.

She'd never trust him. She'd never like him. And she'd certainly never admit to finding him attractive. She was glad it was Giulietta marrying him, not her.

Yet, to be sure, there was nothing like him in Saardova.

Unless you counted the heroic marble nudes that graced the statuary niches in the piazzas and fountains back home.

His formidable physique was clearly made for warfare. But she refused to take any notice of his physical perfection. Under that polished gleam and impeccably tailored dark blue uniform coat, the man was still a Viking-bred barbarian.

Poor Giulietta.

Her Highness seemed nonplused. Giulietta offered her betrothed a begrudging curtsy; Minerva and the rest of ladies-in-waiting followed suit.

They kept their heads down and stayed silent. All the girls remained veiled, of course.

"Your Highness, I bid you welcome to our home," Prince Tor announced in clipped tones formal enough to match his ramrod, military posture. "Thank you for agreeing to our treaty. I look forward to familiarizing you with your new people and your new home once the marriage has been settled."

What poetry! Minerva mentally scoffed. *Well done. You really know how to sweep a lady off her feet. Did you practice that little speech for long? Or did your advisers write it for you?*

"My thanks for your mercy on our people," Giulietta replied, just as the ambassador had instructed, except that her tone bristled with haughtiness.

Tor's eyebrow lifted.

Minerva caught the glint of cynical amusement in his eyes when he looked at his spoiled bride-to-be.

He smiled at Giulietta with cool, knowing indulgence.

It was then Minerva realized rather uneasily that this warlord was a man of serious intelligence and exquisite self-control. She remembered her father's warning. *Prince Tor had the chance to kill me when I was on the ground; he did not. Remember that.* Maybe Papa was right.

Tor could have smashed Saardova into ruins but had chosen not to—and yet, here was the princess whose city and clan he had spared, treating him like some muddy farmhand.

Here was a man, she got the feeling, who was not going to be blinded by Giulietta's beauty once he saw just how beautiful she *was* beneath that veil.

Minerva glanced over at her friend, suddenly wondering if this was the perfect man for Giulietta, after all. One look at that hard face made it clear he was not going to put up with any nonsense. The royal brat may have just met her match. And from the look of things, she didn't like it.

"*W*ell, that wasn't as awful as I'd expected," Tor said that night to his closest friend and fellow soldier, Rolf, after the first meeting with his exotic bride and her people in the great hall. "I'd say it all went smoothly enough."

"Yes, but what does she look like under that veil?" Rolf retorted as he poured them both a draught of vodka. "Wouldn't show her face, I hear. That can't be a good sign."

Tor smirked at him. "That's just their custom. An unmarried young lady of high birth does not appear unveiled to any male outside her own family."

"Wonder why!"

"Apparently, it's to avoid tempting the lusts of Saardovan men."

"Ah, they wouldn't be able to control themselves?" Rolf drawled in amusement.

"Apparently not."

"Well, I hope that's all it is and that your bride doesn't look like a monkey under those seductive, shimmering veils."

He clinked glasses with him ruefully. "I'll find out soon enough."

𝒯hat night in the opulent apartments assigned to the princess and her ladies, everyone was tired from the long day's journey. Fatigue had done nothing to dispose Giulietta to embrace her fate. If anything, it had only made it worse. "I hate it here. He's terrifying."

"You did not think him beautiful?" one of the other ladies whispered.

Giulietta fixed her with a quelling stare. She dropped her gaze and mumbled an apology.

Minerva did her best to soothe her fretful mistress, sitting down beside her a little apart from the others and offering a sisterly hug. "It's going to be all right," she assured the younger girl. "He will give you strong, healthy children. At least there can be no question of that."

She scoffed with a look of disgust. "I don't want that beast to touch me. Who does he think he is?"

Minerva strove for patience, she knew better than to try to speak to her of duty. "You'll get used to him before long. I'm sure he has a good side. You just have to find it. Be patient. One day at a time."

Giulietta frowned.

"Try to smile, dearest," she cajoled her. "Tomorrow is your wedding day!"

Giulietta shrugged Minerva's hand off her shoulder and rose. "I'm going to bed."

Everyone curtsied as the Princess Royal retired.

The ladies exchanged a look that silently agreed her attitude had not made things any easier. Then the Saardovan maids saw to their final duties and wearily bedded down for the night.

Exhausted as she was, Minerva could not fall asleep for the longest time thinking of all the details of the wedding tomorrow. Something she had seen tonight in Giulietta's eyes worried her, a glitter of anger, a flash of hard resolve, almost as if the princess had something up her sleeve.

No doubt, Giulietta had noticed that her future husband was not the sort of man she would twist around her little finger. But the very strength that Minerva had seen in Prince Tor gave her a cautious, newfound hope that someone else might eventually take over her long-held responsibility as Giulietta's minder—namely, him.

This just might work, after all, she mused. Who could say? A bit of structured Rydalburg discipline might be good for the brat. If Giulietta got settled into her new life more quickly than expected, then maybe *she* could return home to her father's villa and take up her classes in the autumn, just as she had planned.

At last, she drifted off to sleep, but her dreams were uneasy that night, haunted by a pair of stern blue eyes . . . and sculpted, but unsmiling lips.

"*W*ake up, wake up! Lady Minerva!"

Someone was shaking her. Someone who was sobbing.

"Oh, please, hurry, Minerva, we need you!"

"What?" Drawn from the depths of sleep and still groggy, Minerva opened her eyes and sat up in bed, still blinking in confusion.

Chaotic noises from the other room registered. Though barely awake, she jumped to her feet and hurried out into the sitting room, where she found the maids and the other ladies-in-waiting running about in a state of hysteria and crying.

"What's wrong? What's going on?" she exclaimed.

"She's gone! She's gone!"

"*What?*"

"We cannot find the princess! Giulietta's missing!"

Minerva looked at them in horror. She clapped a hand over her mouth and felt her stomach plunge all the way to her feet. But there was no time for panic. And there was no one else here to take charge. She lowered her hand from her mouth, but she felt slightly dizzy at this news, and was still not entirely awake. "Are you sure?"

"See for yourself! Her room is empty!"

She marched across the sitting room and flung herself into the doorway to the opulent bedchamber the bride had been assigned.

Empty. She gasped at the confirmation. Yet for a moment longer, she could do naught but stare in disbelief at the empty bed where Her Highness was supposed to be waking up to her wedding day. As if a part of her hoped her friend might magically reappear and this was all a bad dream.

It wasn't. The evidence was real. There was barely a dent in the pillow, nor a wrinkle on the coverlet. The splendid white wedding gown hung waiting on a metal maiden-form—abandoned.

Meanwhile, the maidservants ran about the gilded apartment, wailing in a panic. "Gone, gone! She is gone! The Horse Danes will blame us! We're all going to die!"

"No, we're not." Minerva clutched her chest, leaned in the doorway, and struggled to think what to do. But she had an awful feeling they were right. "Has anyone seen her since last evening? Did anyone hear anything during the night?"

"No, nothing, my lady!"

"Who could have done this?" one of the others sobbed. "Cursed Rydalburgers! What sort of fiend would steal away our poor princess before her wedding? To wreck the treaty?"

"Don't be daft. The little henwit ran away," Minerva growled. Shaking off her daze at last, she marched over to the door that joined the apartment to the rest of the castle. She was in such a state that she almost forgot to veil her face before stepping out into the marble corridor to speak to the Saardovan royal guards stationed there.

In low tones, Minerva explained the situation to their captain, Diego, a loyal soldier who had long served under her father. Diego turned ashen when he heard the news. There was no time for the hundred stunned questions that flashed in his dark eyes—nor had she any answers.

"We must not let the Horse Danes know there is anything amiss. Just find her and bring her back. You have three hours before the wedding."

"Do you think you can buy us some time?"

"Possibly," she answered. "While you ride out

to search the town, I'll dispatch the maids to look for her inside the castle, though I fear she's long gone by now."

"What will you do, my lady?"

"I am going to stay here to head off the prince if the need arises. Maybe she'll come back of her own free will. But if she doesn't"—she swallowed hard—"this marriage will happen one way or the other, Diego," she said grimly. "I am not letting her plunge our people back into war. I promised my father I'd see this treaty through. And the House of Messina always does its duty," she added rather bitterly.

Diego gave her an uneasy nod. "Yes, my lady." Then he pivoted to his men and clipped out a command to follow, leaving only two behind to guard the door. Appearances, after all, had to be upheld.

The proud, cold Horse Danes would not countenance this insult if they found out the royal bride had fled.

Some thanks for their show of mercy—which, from the barbarians, was unprecedented, truth be told. Minerva knew her people should be grateful, but of course, Giulietta had never been grateful a day in her life.

As the soldiers marched off behind Diego, she

retreated into the apartment and brushed back her veil, turning to the maids. They had calmed down a bit now that she had taken control. She gave them their instructions; they donned their veils and padded out silently into the castle to search for their missing royal pain in the bottom. Minerva, left alone in the apartment, shivered in the morning's chill so common to this alien land.

She pulled her silk wrap more tightly round her shoulders. Then she sat down by the window, as if she might be able to see her sunny homeland if she stared hard enough, but it was too far away.

By the gods, how could Giulietta do this? Never mind the practical facts of how she had managed to slip out in the night! Did the pampered beauty think she could actually survive out there without her servants and her guards?

Waited on hand and foot since the day she was born, she barely knew how to pour herself a glass of water.

And where did the little ninny imagine she might go? In spite of her fury, Minerva was worried to death about the royal brat out there on her own. *Spoiled, craven coward.* Still, she couldn't help feeling that this was, to some degree, her own fault. How could she have missed it?

After so many years as her lady-in-waiting, Minerva thought she knew all the princess's tricks by now. But even she had never anticipated that Giulietta might do anything this selfish. *Oh, Papa, why did I ever agree to come here?*

A pang of homesickness moved through her.

The first hour dissolved away into nothing, and still no word from Diego. The maids returned after the second hour. No sign of her in the castle. What were they to do?

Dry-mouthed, Minerva watched the clock hands inch down inexorably to the half-hour mark, and then, at last, she stood. Her face ashen, she glanced at the other ladies.

"Will you help me dress?" she forced out, her usually firm voice little more than a whisper. "The treaty must be saved at all costs."

They nodded in dread-filled resolve.

Filing into the other chamber, they took the royal wedding gown and veil down off the pegs where they were hanging. While one girl sorted out the veil and another set the gauzy white masterpiece of a gown on the bed, Minerva began to undress, her hands shaking.

She could not believe she was going to do this, but she had no choice. Before the mirror, the women worked together to carry out the deception, while somewhere in the palace, Prince Tor waited for his bride.

The day unfolded as a kind of dream. A carriage drawn by six white horses with plumes on their heads brought her to the cathedral. The bells clamored; a rain of confetti and flower petals filled the air; and a deafening thunder of cheers rose from a joyous populace. All across Rydalburg, and even down in Saardova, the ordinary people celebrated the peace of this wedding alliance.

As the carriage halted in front of the cathedral, Minerva couldn't believe the honor Giulietta had chosen to forfeit in doing this service for her people.

As half a dozen dashing uniformed officers from the prince's own regiment assisted her and her ladies down from the carriage, Minerva turned back and blew the crowd a kiss. The cheers grew even louder.

She smiled in spite of the fear of what might happen to her when all this came unraveled, but bracing herself, she headed into the cathedral with her frightened bridesmaids in tow. She herself was to have been the maid of honor, not the bride, of course, but she played her part with dignity despite the *slight* change of plans.

She held on tightly to her composure and glided forward, determined to set the example for the other girls. Hidden behind their pink veils, the other bridesmaids' faces were pale with dread. All were wondering if she'd really get away with this, and what on earth had happened to the real princess.

There was no time for self-doubt as dignitaries from all the surrounding lands bowed to the imposter bride.

Minerva nodded back with what she hoped looked like regal self-possession. Meanwhile, the entire aristocracy of Rydalburg filled the pews. Lords and ladies craned their necks to get a look at her when she came to stand at the back of the cathedral.

Her heart thudded like it might break right out of her chest; she clutched her bouquet and refused to fidget, waiting for her cue.

Holding very still, she fixed her gaze on the tall, powerfully built warrior standing at the front of the church. The pale sunlight streaming through the rose window illumined his long, blond hair and danced on the gold epaulets on his wide shoulders.

Silently, she gulped. Of course she was terrified at the prospect of deceiving such a man. The stern, magnificent barbarian could kill her with one blow if he ever had a mind to.

But this was also a moment of strictest honesty. For she could not say she was not attracted to him.

In blind faith, she had no choice but to keep putting one foot in front of the other as she set out on her long march down the aisle, refusing to look back.

Prince Tor stared at her as she joined him in front of the Bishop of Rydalburg. Then the ordeal of marrying him began in earnest.

Somehow she found the presence of mind to force out the appropriate answers as the Bishop asked each question in turn. Did she pledge herself to this man in loyalty until death? She braced herself with a last mental curse for Giulietta, and bravely gave her word: "I do."

Rings were exchanged; the Bishop joined their hands in matrimony and spoke his final blessing. Then Prince Tor turned to her and with the Bishop's smiling nod of permission, took hold of the lower edges of her veil.

Minerva trembled deep in her very core as the towering blond warrior captured the lacy edges of her veil and lifted it over her head, letting it waft gracefully down her back.

He stared at her for a second, his gaze traveling over her face with a look of fascination. She watched him anxiously, unsure if he was pleased with her or not—or if he had instantly seen through her deception.

What if his spies had somehow found out what the real princess looked like? She could not read him.

But then he offered her a courteous smile of re-assurance. He laid his white-gloved hands on her shoulders and leaned down to kiss her.

She shut her eyes abruptly as he pressed his lips to hers amid thundering applause.

It was the first time any man besides her own blood kin had ever seen her face, let alone touched her, claimed her lips. *Oh, my.*

It was then she knew she was truly in over her head. The thunderous cheering was so loud as he went on kissing her that she marveled the reverberations did not break the stained glass windows. His kiss lasted another few seconds: deliberate but restrained; chaste, polite, as cool as a mountain evening.

How the lusty Prince Orsino would have laughed at him for this studied, schoolboy peck.

But Minerva understood. It was a kiss Tor only gave from duty. Her heart sank a bit. When he ended the kiss and straightened up again—glorious specimen—she was suddenly inspired with a strategy for how she might survive this.

In all likelihood, it was only a matter of time before her charade was uncovered. Impersonating royalty usually spelled death. But there was one way she might be able to mitigate the prince's coming wrath.

That kiss made her wonder if Tor was used to the half-frigid nature of Rydalburg women. So she had heard. Perhaps the famous sensuality of the Saardovans would be her salvation. If she could enthrall her northern prince as a man, bind him to her with pleasure and seduction the likes of which he'd never had, then even the great barbarian might find himself unable to punish her to the full extent of the law for her deception. He might just spare her life.

While these thoughts churned in her head and the prospect of it began to heat her blood, Tor took her hand, turning her to face their audience.

She reached habitually for the covering of her veil, but he stopped her with a gentle touch. "No, my wife, do not hide your beauty from my people," he instructed. "That is not our custom. Besides, once a Saardovan lady is married, she is allowed to show her face. Is it not so?"

She stared at him in surprise, shocked by the big brute's gentlemanly tone and his obvious familiarity with Saardovan ways. In truth, she was even more distracted by the strangeness of having this stranger tell her what to do.

But she nodded warily. "You are correct, my Prince. It was merely habit. I meant no offense."

"None taken." With a guarded smile, he caught her hand between his own and lifted it to his lips, bestowing a quick kiss. "I daresay it is time for our old habits to change—for all of us." His pointed look informed her he was speaking of their people's tradition of warfare.

To show him she wholeheartedly agreed that it ended now, she clasped his big, strong hand more firmly. Tor gave her a subtle nod, reaffirming their newly forged union. Then he led her down the endless aisle of the cathedral.

*A*t the wedding feast that followed, Minerva had no choice but to accept the lavish praise of the people as her due. She nodded her thanks with what she hoped resembled regal self-possession, and soon forgot all about Princess Giulietta.

There were toasts and songs and speeches, and in all, the only person who seemed suspicious was Queen Ingmar, the mother of the groom. The Queen gave Minerva a piercing stare that worried her greatly. But if Her Majesty had an inkling of the switch that had been made, she did not utter a word about it.

Perhaps, as a mother, she, too, wanted an end to the killing above all else.

Then came the entertainments. First, in the

cleared, empty center of the vast banquet hall was a performance of the elite Horse Danes. The cavalry officers in shiny plumed helmets streamed out in formation on their white prancing stallions. The horses seemed to dance to the clipped, measured music, enchanting the crowd with the equine version of a ballet.

They wove through an array of symmetrical formations with stunning precision. Minerva watched in wonder. It was like nothing she had ever seen. The riders made the horses leap in midair and then freeze, balanced on their hind legs while another row swirled by. Others marched to and fro, lifting their front hooves high with every stride while their necks flexed handsomely. Four of the horses spun, while others crisscrossed the open space with mischievous jumps, kicking out their back legs.

At the end of their performance, the riders lined up before the wedding table and finished with a bow, the horses bending down on their front legs. Charmed, Minerva applauded enthusiastically. Her ladies followed suit. And then it was the Rydalburgers' turn to be treated to a performance typical of the lowland culture.

The lights were dimmed to add theatrical flair; colored lanterns were quickly raised around the edges of the stage. As the Saardovan musicians set the mood with a pizzicato on their strings, down from the ceiling were lowered two trapezes and half a dozen long streamers of strong, colorful silk.

On these silken streamers the male acrobats descended, naked from the waist up, their arms, chests, and backs glittered with pearl dust. They were the finest aerial acrobatic dancers in Saardova. They swung on the silks, flipped and flew and leaped from place to place. Minerva enjoyed their marvelous stunts, thumbing their noses at gravity.

Most Saardovan youngsters played on the giant ribbons called silks at some point in their childhood. Doting Saardovan parents hung them from trellises and trees for their young acrobats to swing on, but it took years of dedicated practice to do the daring feats these artists displayed.

Even Minerva winced now and then, watching them, certain one of them would fall and break his neck. The Rydalburgers barely seemed to know what to make of the performance. The crowd gasped each time the acrobats seemed they would surely collide in midair. Then the performers raised the stakes with their favorite stunt: juggling fire.

"They're mad," Tor said with a low laugh as the men tossed burning torches through the air.

Princess Katarina was staring at the half-naked male bodies, wide-eyed.

When the acrobats were finished, the carnival clown skipped out to delight the serious Rydalburg children with his spoofs and illusions. He beckoned a small boy onto the stage to help him find out what was in his brightly painted box. The boy dutifully assisted, then shook his head at the clown. "There's nothing in there, sir."

The clown frowned with exaggerated sorrow and showed the audience the boy was quite correct. The box was empty.

All of a sudden, the illusion was unleashed as half a dozen white doves came fluttering out of it.

Minerva smiled—the symbol of peace. She glanced at Tor and saw that he recognized the meaning of the trick. Everyone applauded, and as the clown retreated with a bow, King Hakon rose and lifted his gold goblet for a toast. "To my son. Tor, you have opened a new chapter in our people's history. Hear, hear!"

Minerva lifted her glass to her new husband, as well. He smiled modestly and nodded at everyone in appreciation. Minerva gazed at him a moment longer than she probably should; he glanced over and met her stare, and they both seemed to forget what they were about. A thrilling spark of word-

less speculation passed between them at the prospect of the night ahead.

Once darkness had descended, fireworks were
set off from the highest mountaintop so that the
people for many miles around could enjoy their
brilliance. As the bright, wondrous colors illumi-
nated the night sky, countless hearts must have
thanked the gods that for once, the booming
noises across the land weren't cannon fire.

Minerva caught a sudden glimpse of a weary,
dusty Captain Diego in the crowd. At a time like
this, she was grateful he did not risk coming to
speak to her privately about their delicate situation. But he shook his head discreetly to signify
they still hadn't found the runaway princess.

She nodded back at him in subtle thanks for
this grim news. It seemed like she would have to
go through with the wedding night, after all. Give
her virginity to the man who had cut off her father's leg. *Oh, help.*

It wasn't much longer after that that Tor captured her hand in the velvet darkness of the night
and looked into her eyes. Sparing her maiden
modesty from public laughter, he drew her away
alone with him while the rest of the world remained dazzled by the fireworks.

Heart pounding, she offered no resistance. *Enthrall him with pleasure?* She scoffed at herself. This

was her first time. She barely even knew what she was doing.

He took her to his chamber and softly closed the door. "I hope you will be comfortable in your new home, my lady."

"Oh—I'm sure I will."

"I'll try not to make this too unpleasant on you."

"P-pardon?"

"I am a-a large man," he said awkwardly. Her eyes widened as she realized what he was talking about. "I will try to do it quickly to minimize any discomfort you might feel."

She stared at him, frozen.

"Bloody hell, I'm already botching this, aren't I?"

Words escaped her.

"It's just I know you're a virgin, and I'm sure you already think me a barbarian, so I just wanted to try to assure you before all this begins that Rydalburg men put their wives up on a pedestal." He faltered and stared at her imploringly, and Minerva was shocked, utterly shocked by the honesty, even the vulnerability, in his eyes. "I come from a warrior people, you know that. But you must also know I will always treat you with the utmost respect."

She studied him in awe. Why, his earnest struggle to find the words to comfort her and allay her fears were more potent on her than the charm of ten suave, cocky Prince Orsinos.

"I won't bother you too much—if you are at all concerned about your, um . . . duties." He nodded discreetly toward the bed.

"Thank you, my lord." Minerva lowered her head, blushing scarlet and trying not to laugh. He was adorable. She had not expected this for a second. "Thank you for that kind reassurance." She could not resist glancing up at him from beneath her lashes, still holding back a laugh. "You need not be embarrassed, sir. I will comply with your wishes."

"Embarrassed? I'm not embarrassed!" The quick denial sounded even more awkward and chagrined, especially as his cheeks flushed.

She tilted her head and looked at him. *No. It can't be.* Surely he wasn't a virgin, too.

"I'm trying to be as considerate as possible, that's all," he insisted. "Because let's put our cards on the table—I know you didn't want this for your life. You don't even know me."

"I'd like to," she answered softly after a heartbeat, and to her own surprise, she meant it. She offered him a tentative smile, more intrigued by him than ever. "Maybe you're not an unfeeling barbarian, after all, my lord."

He relaxed at the gentle barb. "And maybe

you're not a lazy, temperamental hedonist," he whispered with a rueful smile.

"Sometimes," she admitted.

Amusement mingled with a gathering smolder in his eyes as he leaned down to kiss her. His hands grasped her hips.

She reached up to embrace him, threading her fingers at his nape, but as his kiss deepened, she realized she had been mistaken. He was no innocent. He was just being extra careful with her because she was his bride.

It was supposed to be Giulietta, her conscience tweaked her. A part of her felt like she had stolen her friend's man. But it was Giulietta's choice to run away. Besides, if the princess were here right now in her place, she'd probably be crying. To hell with Giulietta, she thought, pulling the great barbarian closer.

Tor began undressing her, and she could not hold herself back from touching him, in turn. She ran her fingers down his cheek, caressed his thick, silky hair, then kneaded his magnificent shoulders while he unlaced the ribbons on her gown. She unfastened his coat and felt his hands tremble as he peeled away her bodice.

Soon they were both naked in the candlelight. Minerva traced the intricate ink designs that adorned the right side of his chest and curled up over his shoulder to spiral around his massive biceps. She had heard that the north men tattooed their bodies with runes and braided Celtic knots, but she had never seen one before. It fascinated her.

"What does it mean?" she murmured.

"It's complicated . . . and I don't feel like talking." He lowered his head to kiss her nipples one by one. She quivered with pleasure, sucking in her breath.

He lifted his head again and looked into her eyes, very much a barbarian, but perhaps a barbarian was exactly what she needed at the moment. She took his mouth violently in an all-consuming kiss. It was useless. Her Saardovan nature took over. She could not get enough of him. His smooth skin blazed to the touch as she caressed him everywhere, his sculpted abdomen, his broad back, his neck. She even dared to graze her fingertips along the tremendous part of him he had warned her about.

Tor gave her a very wicked smile. In turn, he feasted on her neck and earlobe while his fingers stroked between her legs. Minerva was soon panting, bucking with surrender as he pleasured her. His hands were all over her, but his blue eyes were wild and savage as he pressed her onto her back with an unyielding touch and covered her with his body. Minerva's heart thundered like the echo of the fireworks as she spread her legs and gave herself to him.

And when he took her, thrusting in deeply, she cried out just a little, half in pleasure as with pain.

They both paused. There was no turning back now. He kissed her cheek with unexpected sweetness. A moment later, he was back in motion, taking what was his, claiming the spoils of his victory in battle. His blond hair hung around her face as he rocked her; her long, black tresses were strewn across his pillow. Her tanned, olive skin was darker than his as she splayed her hand against his muscled chest and raked him with her nails. He winced with bliss at her rough affections. Then he gripped her buttocks in his hands and simply ravished her, until both of them were motionless, panting.

They lay in spent silence afterwards, their chests heaving. They looked at each other in amazement. Tor looked slightly incredulous—and thoroughly sated. At least for now. "You know," he panted at length, "this might work out even better than I'd hoped."

She laughed in spite of her distant dread of what might happen if and when her charade was uncovered. But at least her plan was working. She closed her eyes and hugged him. *Might as well enjoy it while it lasts.*

*T*he next day, Captain Diego managed to slip a note to Minerva with the latest information. *"We have a lead. A witness saw a girl of her description trying to blend in among the Gypsies."*

The Gypsies! Minerva thought. *So that's how she slipped out of town.*

"Apparently they came into the town to make some money playing music and such in the public celebration after the wedding. They left last night. It shouldn't be long now. They can't have gone far. What do you want me to do with her when we find her?"

She wrote back instructing him to take her back to Saardova, maintaining secrecy. *"Bring her to my father. He'll know what to do."*

She entrusted one of the other ladies with her note and sent it back to him, then went on playing her part.

Guilt gnawed endlessly at her, but unsure where all of this was leading, she had no choice. What was done was done, and she was certainly not about to let the truth come out when the castle remained full of her husband's highborn wedding guests.

It was bad enough that she had deceived him. If he also had to worry about saving face in front of his friends and kinsmen, the consequences for *her* would only be worse.

While Diego went off trying to find the band of Gypsies, Minerva proceeded with her charade in the castle.

She was dimly aware that her feelings for Tor were growing apace with every hour that passed, especially when they made love each night and sometimes even during the day. Every time their bodies joined, it brought their hearts closer. She feared she was falling hopelessly in love with him, this man she had been so determined to hate. But she felt helpless to stop it. There was so much more to him than she had ever expected. He was nothing like the cold, mindless killing machine she had believed him to be before she had actually met him. How could she have known? He was kind; he was loyal; he was incredibly patient, especially with his father, who was none of these things. What would he say if he knew how she was deceiving him? It went beyond a problem of politics now.

Her love would surely hate her if he knew the truth, that she had made a fool of him. He would banish her from his life—and that would break her heart.

She tried not to think about it, staying focused on advancing her course, now that she had committed to it. Maybe she could simply become the Giulietta everybody thought she was. He introduced her by that name to his friends, of course. They were all sitting around in the afternoon doing nothing in particular. She gathered from their jests that this was not normal Rydalburg behavior.

"You Saardovans are having an influence on us," his officer friends from his regiment teased her.

"What, teaching you how to relax?" she drawled.

"Don't look at me! I'm a shy virgin!" Rolf mimicked a high-pitched feminine voice, drawing his handkerchief across his face like a veil.

Tor punched him; he went flying off his chair in a gale of laughter. His companions began regaling her with stories about her new husband, like the time Tor had rescued a peasant who had fallen through the ice on a frozen river crossing.

At length, another rogue named Ivar tricked her into tasting a swallow of some strong traditional Rydalburg whiskey.

She coughed at the fiery stuff, and in return, dared the hearty northern braggart to try eating a Saardovan hot pepper.

He actually did it, though his face turned crimson and tears ran from his eyes. Ivar stomped his feet in protest at the pain he had subjected himself to while the others laughed heartily and mocked him.

"Right. Give me one of those," Tor commanded the servant who had brought out the peppers.

"You're going to regret it," she warned, but he looked at her with a playful challenge sparkling in his eyes, then he popped the whole thing into his mouth.

Minerva shook her head as the rest of his men (save Ivar) followed their prince, subjecting themselves to the same punishment. She ate one of the pepper slices casually, then another, tossing it into the air and catching it in her mouth, while the great warriors writhed in pain and begged for water.

*T*he next day, Tor escorted her out to the royal stables, where the revered Lippizan horses lived in splendor.

They watched the babies skipping around the meadow with their dams. Leaning on the fence, she was intrigued to see that the foals were actually born black and then turned white as they matured. Tor explained the steps they went through in their training to be able to do such tricks on command by the time they were full grown.

But on that sun-warmed spring afternoon, he gave her a certain look, and the next thing she knew, the newlyweds were in the hayloft.

Another day passed. She had the opportunity to take a stroll with her new sister-in-law, Princess Katarina. Minerva soon realized that Kat, as her brother called her, was as cautious and circumspect a princess as Giulietta was emotional and dramatic.

"You've certainly brightened things up around here," she said shyly as the two walked arm in arm in the garden.

"Have I?"

"You have! Now everyone is cheerful. Even Mama."

"Really?" She had been taking care to give Queen Ingmar a wide berth, for she had the uneasy feeling that Tor's mother completely saw through her.

Kat nodded. "It was always so gloomy around here before you came and married my brother. Maybe because of the war. I'm just glad it's over."

"I am, too."

"Are you very homesick?" Kat asked sweetly.

"A little," she admitted.

"Well, if there's anything I can do to make you

feel more at home here, just say the word."

"How dear you are!" Minerva exclaimed, giving her a half-hug, an arm around her shoulders. Such affection seemed surprising to the princess, but she smiled, blushing a little. Minerva quite adored the demure creature.

"My brother seems quite smitten with you," Kat remarked as they strolled on.

"I have to admit the feeling is mutual."

"I'm so happy to hear that! He is a wonderful big brother. But I hear you have a brother, too. It must have hurt your feelings that he wouldn't come to your wedding."

It took Minerva an extra split second to realize Kat was talking about Orsino. "Oh, yes, well, defeat was hard enough for him to bear. Watching me marry Tor would have been more than he could swallow. It's better he stayed home, believe me. He's a bit of a hothead. He probably would have started causing trouble. He always does."

Kat looked askance at her. "Is he really as handsome as everybody says?"

"He certainly thinks so!" Minerva replied, and both girls laughed. "Come, tell me something about your brother that I don't know."

"Hmm . . . Did you know he has a green thumb?"

"Really?"

"Come this way, I'll show you."

Kat hurried her back to the castle and led the way to a conservatory that opened up off one of the wings of the palace that she had not yet visited.

"Why, it's just like being back in Saardova!" she breathed as she stepped through the white metal-framed door into the warm, humid air beneath the fanciful glass dome.

"Tor calls this winter garden," Kat explained. "He gives Mother and me roses in the dead of January."

Minerva was amazed. There were little orange and lemon trees in pots. Surely he had imported them from her homeland. There were mounds of pink flowers hanging from pots, an indoor grape arbor, and a fountain where oversized goldfish swam lazily. Containers sprouted neatly labeled medicinal herbs. She knew them well, considering she had once planned to study to become a doctor.

Shaking her head, she was so stunned by this discovery that she barely heard Kat prattling away. "Of course, Father makes fun of my brother constantly about his garden, but Tor says when he's king he'll never let our people starve. Or our horses. Come and see his experimental food crops." Kat beckoned her over to a long, rectangular section by the wall where an assortment of vegetables grew. Behind them stood a row of different grasses and grains.

If there was any doubt left, Minerva took one look at this project and knew she had fallen in love with the man.

"He's tried grafting different species of food plants so the corn will be more hardy and the turnips and such can better resist disease. You see, unlike Saardova, much of Rydalburg has rocky and difficult soil. Our climate can be very unforgiving. Tor says a couple of harsh winters in a row is all it would take to push our people to the brink of starvation. Then our warriors would be too weak to fight so we could gain better territory."

Minerva turned to her in shock. "Is that the real reason our two countries have so often gone to war? My people dread the thought of running out of fresh water, like you have in all these mountain streams, while yours live in fear of insufficient food?"

Kat considered this. "I think you may be right. Look at this." Then his obviously devoted sister turned away, gazing at his handiwork. "It's a wonder, isn't it?"

And so is he, she thought, nodding.

"*G*owe you an apology, Giulietta," Tor said, quite out of the blue, as they sat on the balcony that evening sharing a bottle of wine. The stars were popping out one by one as the light faded from the sky. Night birds began to warble.

Minerva looked at her husband curiously. "How's that?"

"I fear I've done you a disservice by even listening to the whispers from your kingdom," he admitted with a rueful half smile. "You are nothing like my spies said you'd be."

"Really?" she asked in a guarded tone. *I can imagine.* "What did they say?"

He studied the mountain view for a moment, debating on whether or not to tell her. Then he shrugged. "I hate to pass along idle gossip, but in this case, I'll make an exception. Because somehow, a lot of people back in Saardova seem to have the wrong impression about you."

"Do tell."

"I'm afraid they call you selfish and spoiled. Temperamental. Prone to tantrums."

"Me?" she forced out, laughing.

He nodded. "I admit, I was a little worried. I heard the only person who can keep you in check is Messina's daughter, your lady-in-waiting."

"Oh, that's an exaggeration." She scoffed, but was having trouble looking him in the eyes.

"Of course," he conceded. "Idle talk, as I said. Still, I'd like to meet this friend of yours sometime."

Minerva went even more on guard. "Why?"

"I believe she and I have a mutual acquaintance—besides your lovely self," he added, toasting her with his glass.

"Who?" she asked, fairly holding her breath to hear his answer.

"The old scholar, Montevecchio. I hear he's now the dean of the University of Saardova. He must be what, ninety by now? I imagine he's the one behind your friend being accepted as the first female student. He has peculiar views."

He was right, but she was astonished. "How on earth do you know Montevecchio or his peculiar views?" she exclaimed.

"Everyone knows Montevecchio," he teased.

"Tor!" She stretched out her leg to poke him with her toe. "Tell me, you ruffian!"

"He was once my tutor."

Minerva stared at him in shock. "You had a Saardovan tutor?"

She had heard that the old sage had gone traveling all around Europe ages ago.

"He showed up here when I was just a lad. Said he had come to study our ways."

"I can't believe he came here! Your father—"

"Thought he was a spy, yes." Tor shook his head. "He had the world-famous scholar thrown into the dungeon and tortured every day . . . until Father realized his mistake. Hakon's treatment of the great philosopher was a huge embarrassment to Rydalburg. So Father sought to make it up to him, gave him a plum post here for a while."

"I knew nothing of this!"

"He probably avoided talking about it back in Saardova for fear of fanning the flames of war. Thankfully, the old man found it in his heart to forgive my father for his brutality. My mother made sure our author friend was treated from that point on as an honored guest. Montevecchio was given his own quarters in the keep for his private study. I loved going to visit him up in the tower room . . . see all his books, hear his ruminations. He had a perspective on things unlike anyone else I knew."

Minerva gazed at him, marveling.

"He stayed with us two years. And just between you and me, my darling, I've always suspected that I was the real reason Montevecchio came to Rydalburg. He knew exactly what he was doing."

"What do you mean?"

"As I said, I was just a child, but he knew one day I would be king. He wanted to teach me about your people. To show me that you were . . . good." He paused, lost in his thoughts. "I don't think I ever would've entertained the notion of a treaty uniting our lands if it were not for old Montevecchio."

"Then I owe him greatly," she whispered, leaning closer to kiss him.

Tor pulled her onto his lap. "We both do." He caressed her hair as he pressed his lips to hers. "Would you mind if I ask you an awkward question, Princess?"

She leaned back to peer dubiously into his eyes. "No. What's the question?"

He furrowed his brow, casting about for the words. "Was there—someone else who had your heart before you came here and were forced to marry me?"

"Why, no! No one! Why would you ask such a thing?"

He looked relieved but still uncertain as he slid his arms around her waist. "Because of the distance you put between us."

"I do?"

He nodded. "I can certainly feel it. Not to brag, but distance is not the usual reaction I get from females. Come, you can tell me. I won't be angry. Is there . . . something about me you don't like?"

"Nothing at all!" she exclaimed. "Tor, you're the most wonderful man in the world! Please don't feel that way. I don't understand why you would say that."

"Sorry, I'm botching this. What I'm trying to say is that you can be yourself with me, Giulietta."

She looked away with a wince.

"I don't demand the sort of obedience Saardovan men expect. I want to know you," he said earnestly. "That is all I meant. Don't be upset by my question, please." He captured her chin and turned her face back to meet her fretful gaze. "You fascinate me. I've never known anyone like you. But I can feel you holding back. You don't have to, with me. Surely you know by now that I would never hurt you."

Minerva looked at him in distress. It was everything a girl could wish for a man to say to her. Only, in her case, it was all wrong.

He thought he was saying them to Giulietta. Wretched with tangled longing and guilt, she said not a word but wrapped her arms around him and laid her head on his shoulder.

He embraced her tenderly, running his hands up and down her back. She squeezed her eyes shut, wretched with the knowledge of how she was deceiving him.

She couldn't believe that the so-called barbarian warlord was perceptive enough to notice how she had been holding herself back emotionally. Her poor prince thought she was keeping him at bay because she held some sort of Saardovan grudge against him. The man had no idea she was a fraud. How she loathed herself for this— and loathed Giulietta! She hadn't seen Diego in three days.

He was off hunting for the real princess among the Gypsies. In the meanwhile, Tor seemed very determined to win her heart, unaware that he was wooing an imposter.

When he lowered his head slowly and caressed her lips with his own, it was more temptation than she could stand. She took his chiseled face between her hands and kissed him in aching desire. A beautiful sunset unfurled across the sky, but they did not stay out on the balcony long to admire it. She took him by the hand and drew him wordlessly into their chamber.

There they proceeded to show each other that somehow, indeed, this had quickly developed into much more than a political match. And as he peeled her gown off her shoulders, Minerva half hoped the real Giulietta might never be found.

"*O*h, sister! I have a surprise for you!" Princess Katarina's voice echoed from the corridor beyond the morning room where she and Tor were having breakfast.

Minerva looked over with a curious smile as the blond princess poked her head in the doorway. "Surprise! Your brother's come!"

Prince Orsino stepped into view.

She froze as he flashed a rueful smile. "Lady Minerva. Good to see you again. So where is she?" He glanced around the morning room in question.

Minerva's mind was a blank as both Tor and Kat looked at her in confusion.

"Minerva?" Tor echoed with a decidedly ominous note in his voice.

"He is joking!" she exclaimed, sounding rather shrill as she shot up from her chair. "Of course I'm not Minerva! He's always teasing. You are so silly, brother!" She hurried over to greet Orsino with a sisterly hug.

He furrowed his brow, but smiled as he hugged her back. "Now who's joking? Where's Giulietta?"

Tor suddenly swept to his feet and threw down his breakfast napkin with a curse. "I knew it!"

"What?" Kat murmured.

"Please—I can explain—"

"What's happened? Where is my sister?" Orsino demanded.

"Oh, Hades," she whispered, backing away from him, and backing away from Tor as he stalked toward her, his eyes ablaze.

"What is going on here? You are not the Princess Giulietta?"

"Of course she's not," Orsino retorted.

"I wasn't talking to you," Tor growled.

Minerva gulped. "I can explain."

"Who are you?" her husband demanded.

"Don't yell at her, Tor!"

"Stay out of this, Kat."

Orsino took a step toward him. "What have you done with my sister? Has something happened to Giulietta?"

"Don't try me, Saardovan!" Tor thundered without warning, then he turned back to the cowering Minerva. "Explain yourself," he said icily.

"It's true," she forced out, lowering her head. "I am Lady Minerva de Messina. The general's daughter."

He stared at her incredulously. "Why?"

"Please! I didn't want to deceive you!" she cried, lifting her gaze to meet his imploringly. "The real princess fled the night before the wedding! I promised my father I'd see the treaty through."

"*Fled?*" Tor echoed in fury.

"What do you mean, she fled? Where is she?" Orsino exclaimed.

"I don't know! Her guards have been out looking for her since the morning of the wedding. I dispatched them as soon as we realized she was gone."

"So you thought you'd take her place?" Tor asked in outrage. "How dare you lie to me? You'd make a fool of me in front of both our nations?"

"I was trying to save the treaty!"

He turned away. "Get her out of my sight. Guards! Throw this imposter in the tower. Saardovan treachery! I should have known! Maybe Father was right about you people."

"Tor, please!" she cried as they dragged her away.

"Unhand her!" Orsino ordered. "You have no right to do that to a lady!"

"I have every right," Tor said icily. "The little liar is my wife."

Minerva's heart pounded. The big, blond Rydalburg warriors' hold on her arms was implacable. Try as she might, she could not fight free. As they left the palace proper, she could still hear Tor and Orsino roaring at each other.

All of her pleading with his men had no effect. They were completely expressionless as they half dragged, half carried her up the stone steps of the tower. Before she could collect her thoughts, they deposited her in a room in the highest tower of Rydalburg Castle.

She heard them lock the door. She pounded on it. "Let me out of here!" They ignored her. As it sank in that the stony-hearted guards would not be moved, she turned away, feeling ill. She began to pace the austere stone garret, distraught over hurting Tor. She thought she had made the right decision for the treaty's sake, but now she wondered if she had only made things worse.

And where was Giulietta? Producing the real princess seemed the only hope of fixing this disaster. All she knew from Diego's last message was that the Gypsies were moving north. How hard could it be to find them? He should have been back by now!

An hour later, she heard voices in the stone stairwell outside her garret cell.

"Visitor!" the guard called roughly as he unlocked the door. *Tor? Orsino?* Or might it be Diego, bringing news that he had found the princess?

But when the door opened, Kat stepped in, looking shaken. She lifted her chin, waiting for the guards to close the door behind her.

Minerva's eyes filled with tears of remorse as soon as they were alone. "I'm so sorry—"

"There's no time," she whispered. "I'm not supposed to be here. I insisted the guards grant me a couple of minutes to make sure you're all right." Kat stepped over to the cot with a businesslike air and hitched up one side of her dark velvet skirt, producing one of the aerial silks like those used by the acrobats. "I hope you know how to use this thing. I got it from one of your ladies-in-waiting. I thought of stealing a rope for you, but then they'd know it was I who helped you escape."

"Oh, Kat," she murmured as her sister-in-law handed over the giant ribbon.

"You have to get out of here and find the real Giulietta, or they're going to kill each other. Tor and Prince Orsino."

"What?" she breathed.

"You saw them arguing," Kat said in a hushed, hurried tone. "Well, it escalated after you left, and now they say they're going to settle any future conflicts tonight, not with a marriage between our houses, but by single combat. They're planning a duel to the death!"

Minerva stared at her in horror. "When?"

"Tonight, sunset. There's no time to waste. You have to find the princess and bring her back, Minerva. It's the only thing that will satisfy Orsino—and our only hope of stopping this madness."

She was still reeling at the news while Kat

marched over to the mullioned window and opened it, assessing the height of it with a slight wince. "You'll have to climb down. I think if you lower yourself to that roof, and then down to that lower gable, you can reach the ground from there. I left a horse waiting for you at the bottom of the wall."

"You're brilliant." She hugged her. "Thank you for your help. I'm so sorry for putting you through all this."

"You did it for the treaty. I understand. Besides, I know my brother loves you, and that you love him. I can see it in you both. Whether you planned it or not, you've fallen in love. But I must warn you, Tor does not forgive easily. You have to make this work. If you fail, one of our princes will end up dead, and sure as clockwork, the war will start again by morning." Kat gave her a sudden, sisterly embrace that was quite out of character for any Rydalburg noblewoman.

But the guard knocked again on the door to let her know her time was up.

"Be careful," Kat whispered.

Minerva quickly hid the silk streamer under the cot. Then the blond princess smoothed her hair and glided out as demurely as she had come in.

When the guard had locked the door again, Minerva glanced over at the window and swallowed hard. She had not swung on an aerial in years, and never from such a height. Never for such stakes.

She dragged the bed, the heaviest piece of furniture in the room, as quietly as possible over to the window. Jamming it against the wall so it could not slip, she then threaded the ribbon beneath one leg of the bed and tied the loose ends into a knot, which she fixed right at her waist.

Climbing up onto the windowsill, she felt the high mountain breeze on her cheeks as she peered down at the earth below in a cold sweat. *Here goes nothing.*

Checking her knot one more time, she inched backwards out the window, then pushed off and began walking down the wall, the ribbon cupping her bottom and her back, not unlike the seat of a child's swing. She gripped both sides of the silk streamer and refused to look down as she lowered herself bit by bit.

She prayed no one noticed her. She refused to look down, but if she had glanced earthward, she would have seen there was no one around to see her. It was a nerve-racking ordeal. Her biceps felt shaky by the time she reached the first roof landing.

When her feet stood on its solid surface, she untied the knot at her waist and pulled one end of the silk ribbon free from where it had been looped around the bed above.

It came spilling down from the window above in a tumble of bright fabric. She quickly caught it and repeated the process, this time using an iron gargoyle as her anchor. The second descent was shorter, and before she knew it, she landed breathlessly on the ground. She untied her knot again and pulled the streamer after her, balling it up as she ran to find the horse Kat had promised.

She found the waiting animal tied to a tree just inside the woods across from where she had landed. "Brilliant girl," she murmured, finding the water canteen and spyglass that Katarina had tucked in the saddlebag. Minerva vaulted up onto the horse's back and urged it into motion, heading for the rocky country to the north. She had to find those Gypsies and get Giulietta back to Rydalburg Castle by sunset tonight.

For the next three hours, she urged her horse on through woods, up hills, down valleys, and when she came to a river, she followed it. The royal henwit would at least have the sense to stay close to a water source.

Then Minerva began seeing signs of human life in the lonely landscape. A burnt-out campfire. Bits of garbage on the ground. Cantering up over the rise, she spotted the colorful caravan below. Gypsies!

She lifted the spyglass to her eye, searching their whimsical camp for Giulietta. Somehow the wandering bands of free-spirited Romany folk had managed to stay neutral in all those rashes of conflict between Rydalburg and Saardova. That was not to say that they were necessarily trustworthy. But the Gypsies hadn't gone terribly far from the castle, she thought. Why had Diego not reported finding them?

Puzzled, she rode on toward the camp, though she still had not spotted the runaway princess. Giulietta might be in one of the wagons or even wearing a disguise, she thought. It was hard to tell from this distance. She needed a closer look. She urged her tiring horse into a canter and hastened to catch up with them. After all, the sun was now directly overhead: high noon.

The Gypsies eyed her warily as she rode into their camp and asked to see their leader.

"Who are you and what do you want?" A dashing, dark-eyed fellow swaggered forward, a veritable Gypsy prince.

He was dressed in a dark brocade vest over a loose white shirt, with black trousers and boots. His long, raven hair was messily braided in a queue, tied with a red ribbon. Which Minerva instantly recognized as belonging to Giulietta. *Well, well.*

"I am looking for a lady who I have reason to believe has recently been traveling with you, sir."

"Ah, she wants the troublemaker."

They all started laughing.

"At least you're prettier than the last bunch who came looking for her."

Minerva considered the ribbon in his hair and understood. "She got you to lie to them for her, didn't she?"

"Forgive me if I am not an upstanding citizen. I don't like being told what to do. Not by soldiers to whom I owe no allegiance . . . and not by a fair-faced brat, either."

"I understand, believe me. I'm here to take her off your hands."

He lifted his chin. "And you are?"

"Her best friend. Please, it's very important. Do you have her or not?"

"Who is she?" he evaded. "She certainly seems to think she's someone of consequence."

"You might say that. Suffice to say she's a runaway who left disaster in her wake. It's time for her to go back and face the music, or there will be far-reaching consequences for us all. Please tell me she is safe!"

"More or less. She isn't here," he finally admitted.

Minerva gasped. "Did something happen? Was she hurt?"

"Just her pride," he drawled. Then he gestured toward the hills. "I ordered her out of my camp about an hour ago. We left her by herself back by the caves to the west."

"By herself?"

He scowled. "I couldn't take her tantrums and demands anymore! But of course, I don't wish any harm to befall the chit. She does seem fairly helpless. You'd better go and find her."

"Thank you."

The flamboyant but slightly ragtag leader gave her a bow.

Minerva wheeled her horse around and rode off for rugged higher ground, where caves honeycombed the mountain. Blazes, there were too many of these caves to search. She'd never find her. She debated on whether to try calling for her, because if the princess saw her coming, she might decide to hide. Cantering her horse past more caves, peering into each one, she suddenly heard a familiar voice call to her.

"Minerva!"

She reined in and glanced back over her shoulder. Relief washed through her—and a degree of amusement.

There was the glamorous Giulietta—bedraggled, her silk finery smudged with dirt, her famously beautiful eyes full of misery. Minerva noted the princess had also done away with her veil. As Minerva began riding toward her, Giulietta burst into tears.

"Oh, thank the gods you've come! I've been so wretched—and I'm starving! Please tell me you've brought me something to eat."

"Is that all you have to say for yourself?" Minerva jumped off the horse. "That you're hungry?"

"Well, I am," she said with a pout and a wide-eyed blink, having learned absolutely nothing from her ordeal, it seemed.

Minerva's hands fisted by her sides. "Do you have any idea what you have done?"

"I couldn't go through with it! I'm sorry! But he's too much of a brute!"

"No, he's not! You didn't even give him a chance! You don't know him."

"And you do?"

Minerva glared at her. "I married him for you. No, not for you," she corrected herself. "For our country."

"What?"

"I tried to save the situation, but now everything's gone to the devil and you're the only one who can fix it. You have to come back, Giulietta, you have to. And if you don't agree, by the gods, I will tie you up and drag you from the back of the horse!" she thundered, reaching for the silk streamer to make good on her threat.

"Minerva, you've gone mad!"

"Yes, I have! And who could blame me? As if you're not enough of a pain in the neck, your brother went and ruined everything! Now he and my husband are going to duel to the death unless you come back and take responsibility for your actions! You have no idea the trouble you've left in your wake."

Giulietta frowned. No doubt, she didn't want to hear this, but Minerva's tone conveyed the seriousness of the situation.

"Please, Giulietta. If ever there was a time to act like a true princess, that time is now. You have a duty to your people."

She winced, eyeing Minerva uncertainly. "What would you have me do?"

"Go back and apologize. Let your brother see that the Rydalburgers have not treacherously murdered you, because that's what he's accusing. Then fall to your knees before Prince Tor and beg him to let you carry out the terms of the treaty even now, and pray your beauty has the usual effect."

"What about you?"

Minerva was silent for a moment. "I am probably going to prison."

Giulietta trembled visibly and looked like she might faint. "I've caused all this?"

"Yes."

"Minerva, I never meant for any of this to happen—"

"You never do. There's no time. Come now and make it right."

She pressed her lips together and nodded. "Very well. There is nothing else for me out here, anyway." She cast a wistful glance back in the direction of the Gypsy prince's camp. Then she got up on the horse behind Minerva, and both girls rode back to Rydalburg Castle with all due haste.

*T*hey arrived at the castle minutes before sunset. The girls jumped down from the exhausted horse and raced to the field where the duel was to take place.

Giulietta was a mess, running bareheaded through the crowd of courtiers and military men who had gathered to watch the grim proceedings. The mood in the crowd seemed to drive home to the frivolous princess just how serious the situation was that she had precipitated with her childish disappearance.

Each prince's entourage had gathered around him. They stood making their final preparations on the two opposite ends of the green, north and south, so the sunset in the west would not be in the eyes of either contender.

"Orsino!" Giulietta shouted.

He stopped, looked over, and then yelled her name in answer when he saw her racing through the crowd.

"Don't do this!" She did not stop to talk to him, but went barreling toward the other prince—at least until the guards surrounding him caught her. Two of them grabbed her by the arms.

"What do you want, girl?"

"Please! I need to see Prince Tor!"

"Who are you?" they demanded.

"Let her pass!" Minerva ordered as she came striding up behind her royal friend.

The guards hesitated. They had become accustomed to taking orders from her over the past few days, but of course, the last anyone had heard, she had been locked in the tower.

Tor turned at the sound of her voice and saw both women. His eyes narrowed.

"Please, Tor, hear us out. For Montevecchio's sake," Minerva begged him.

He glowered at her, but dismissed the guards with a nod. "Let them through," he growled.

As soon as the guards released her arms, Giulietta did exactly as Minerva had advised and rushed toward him, dropping to her knees. "Great Prince! Please forgive me! I have failed you, and shamed my people. I am not worthy of you, but if you can find mercy in your heart for a foolish girl's cowardice, I am the real Giulietta and I will uphold the treaty."

The sight of his sister bowing down to the enemy enraged Orsino, who came storming toward them, but Minerva held him back.

"Stop it. For once in your life, think with something other than your ego. Keep your mouth shut!"

"How dare you?"

"Because I know I'm right! You see?" she gestured toward his sister. "Alive and safe, as promised. You owe His Highness an apology for your false accusations."

He glanced back to where Giulietta was still pleading with Tor, kneeling, tears running down her face. "What is she doing?" Orsino demanded.

"She's asking him to let us fix the wrong that has been done him. It's the only way."

Orsino eyed her mistrustfully. "What if he doesn't accept it? If a woman did that to me, I'd spit on her."

"Well, he isn't you," Minerva whispered rather

bitterly. "Besides, I signed Giulietta's name on the marriage license. She could make the claim she's already his legal wife. It just depends on how well the lawyers argue."

Giulietta must have finished her speech, for she had hung her head and awaited her sentence.

Tor glanced past her to where Minerva stood with Orsino.

He dropped his weapon begrudgingly on the ground, but shook his head. "Very well. But you're mad if you think I'll ever have anything to do with Saardovan women again."

That was the moment that little Kat stepped into their midst and put them all to shame.

"I will uphold the treaty," she spoke out.

Everyone looked at her.

"I will marry the Prince Orsino, if he will have me—on the condition that he take no other wife but me."

The whole crowd gasped and Orsino's eyes widened.

Minerva gazed at the northern princess in anguished affection.

"Don't be silly, you can't do that, Katarina," Tor clipped out.

"Yes, I can." She looked at Orsino expectantly.

He seemed amazed.

"Orsino," Minerva said through gritted teeth.

He gave her a slight frown askance.

"You'll never do better than her," she said to him under her breath. "Believe me."

"Funny, before all this, on my way to Rydalburg, I was thinking of marrying you."

Minerva shook her head. "I'm in love with Tor."

"Poor creature. So that's why you don't want me to fight him."

"Well?" Kat demanded, her cheeks coloring as he left her waiting for his answer.

Orsino went to her and bowed with the courtly grace he was famous for. "Your Highness, it would be an honor. I humbly accept, and agree to your condition."

Katarina smiled in relief, but the only one who did not look at all pleased was Tor. Minerva turned to him, aching with the knowledge of how she had hurt him.

Giulietta stood and backed away as she walked over to him slowly. Everyone watched as Minerva approached the man she thought of as her husband, even though she realized the marriage was not legal.

"If you have something to say to me, say it and be gone," he ground out.

Minerva searched his storm-blue eyes imploringly. "I'm sorry. I never meant to hurt you. I only did it for the good of my people and yours. But I understand as prince you are responsible for fulfilling the law." With that, fully expecting to be placed under arrest, she held out her wrists to be shackled.

He glanced down at her hands and then glared at her; he shook his head to signal the guards that she was not to be touched.

But he turned away, refusing to make eye contact with her again. "I want you gone from here, and don't come back."

Minerva flinched, tears rushing into her eyes. But it was too late now. She should have told him the truth before it came to this, she realized too far after the fact.

To avoiding causing any more of a scene, she bowed to him with what remained of her dignity and withdrew. She knew she should be grateful she was allowed to leave with her freedom. Yet her heart was broken to know she would never see him again, and every inch of her body ached with shame as the people she had deceived watched her pass.

She glanced at Katarina sorrowfully as she went by.

The princess touched her hand with a regretful gaze as she passed.

Back in the palace, Minerva fought back tears as she got her things together and bade the royal maids, her coconspirators, farewell.

She assured them Tor would not take revenge on them. However angry he might be, she knew by now the "barbarian" would not harm defenseless women. Then she evacuated her temporary post in favor of its rightful owner.

Tor wanted nothing to do with Giulietta at the moment, but they were already married on paper. Besides, Minerva had seen the power of her friend's charms work on countless males before. Just like that Gypsy prince. Even cold, stony Tor would eventually succumb.

It was only a matter of time.

*T*hree months later, Minerva sat at her desk with her books opened in front. Instead of studying, however, she was gazing wistfully out the window toward the distant mountains, thinking of all that had happened, and the love that she had let slip through her fingers . . .

Upon her return to Saardova, she had cried on her father's shoulder, and then resumed her old life, except for her service as lady-in-waiting. She wasn't needed anymore. Giulietta hadn't come back. So Minerva had started her classes at the university as planned.

She sighed and picked up her pen once more, determined to finish the lesson for this week's class. After all, this was what she had wanted for her life.

A lot had happened in the weeks that had passed. Everyone's lives had changed drastically. Orsino and Katarina were married and madly in love. Giulietta was spending some time in a northern convent, learning contemplation and the service of the poor—particularly the Gypsies.

King Hakon had died of a heart attack in the middle of a feasting. Queen Ingmar was rumored to have entered into a torrid affair with Captain Diego within a fortnight of her difficult husband's funeral.

Tor had become king. Minerva had practically memorized the newspaper article describing his coronation. Things had not worked out between him and Giulietta. The marriage on paper between them had been annulled.

For her part, Minerva was debating on how or even whether to tell His Majesty that she was carrying his child.

Just then, a light knock sounded on her bedroom door.

"Yes?"

She looked over as Papa opened the door and poked his head into her room. "You have a visitor."

She frowned, annoyed that he had climbed the stairs again on his peg leg rather than sending up the maid to give her the message. "I have to study, Papa. Tell them I'm not at home."

"Minerva," he said quietly, "this is someone you're going to want to see."

She furrowed her brow as he pushed the door the rest of the way open; she gasped and jumped to her feet as the King of Rydalburg stepped into view.

Tor's towering stature nearly filled the doorframe.

She stared at him, wide-eyed, her mouth agape. She looked from him to her father, realizing how bizarre this moment was, all things considered. Her father gave her a bolstering look. "I'll leave you two alone."

"Thank you, General," Tor said in his stiff, formal way as he stepped into her room.

Minerva stared at him in amazement as her sire withdrew and pulled the door shut. "What are you doing here?"

"Hmm. I've been wondering that myself." He looked around the room, anywhere but at her. "Please, sit down."

She eased back down into her chair beside her writing table while he stood, fidgeting, in the center of her room.

"Lovely place, Saardova," he remarked. "Glad I didn't destroy it."

"I didn't know you were coming," she forced out.

"Yes. It was, ah, spontaneous on my part. I'm not . . . usually spontaneous, am I?"

She gazed at him in helpless adoration. "I'm sorry about your father."

He nodded with a guarded glance at her. "Thank you."

He hesitated. "Well, I'm just going to say it! What you did was madness. The way you lied to me." He shot her an anguished look, then dropped his gaze. "When Giulietta ran away, you should've just come to me and told me what had happened—but I know now you couldn't. You thought I was an ogre."

"Not an ogre."

"You didn't trust me. And yet you put yourself in my hands. You dared to deceive me . . . for the sake of our people. That means something different to me now than it did when I was just a prince." He held her in a tempestuous stare, as though he had been infected with Saardovan passion. Yet still he struggled for self-control. "You have some nerve, girl. And by nerve, I mean courage. The treaty was more important to you than your own safety." He shook his head, at a loss. "If that is not royal behavior, I don't know what is."

She swallowed hard and lowered her gaze. She could not keep looking into those big, blue eyes of his or she knew she would cry. "Well, you would be the expert on such matters. You are King."

"And I've never been more alone," he said softly.

She looked up again in spite of herself, captured by the heart-tugging admission of vulnerability from the warlord.

His gaze changed, softened. "I came to tell you what you did was madness. But if you hadn't done it, then I never would've got the chance to be your husband."

Her eyes widened as he took a step toward her and then went down on one knee. She drew in her breath as he pulled a diamond ring out of his pocket.

He offered it to her. "Minerva . . . my love, whatever your name is, I want you back. Please be my wife and queen."

Minerva looked at him in wonder, then burst into tears and threw her arms around him, kissing his face and whispering "yes" over and over again.

And now a sneak peek at
Gaelen Foley's exciting new novel

MY NOTORIOUS GENTLEMAN

On sale August 2013

CHAPTER ONE

LONDON, 1816

*G*eorge was foxed, but that, Grace supposed, was to be expected. The carefree young dandy plopped down beside her onto the bench at the perimeter of the ballroom, and declared: "Miss Kenwood, I adore you!"

"Ah, that's very nice, George."

"I mean it, I worship you!"

"Worship God and use your head, dear lad," she answered, surveying the ballroom.

He laughed as though she had said something charming. "Spoken like a true preacher's daughter! I daresay you could save even *my* soul, Miss Kenwood. But 'tis true," he slurred, lifting his glass to her. "You are my ideal woman in all things." He glanced down innocently at her gown. "What you lack in fashion, you make up for with substance!"

She turned to him, startled. "Er, thank you, my lord."

Perfect. Just what she needed to hear. Confirmation from their host's own son that she *looked* as out of place as she felt in the Marquess of Lievedon's opulent Town palace.

Miss Grace Kenwood, firmly on the shelf at the advanced age of five-and-twenty, was not accustomed to aristocratic ballrooms.

Everyone raved about the worldly delights of London, but the sprawling metropolis made her miss her garden. The air in the crowded capital made her skin feel dirty compared to the fresh breezes and sunshine of the countryside.

And the people . . . well, one was not to judge, but suffice it to say these were decadent times.

"What are you doing hiding in the shadows like a wallflower, anyway?" her wayward young friend demanded, bumping her shoulder with his own, like an overgrown schoolboy flirting with his governess.

At twenty-one, George, Baron Brentford, or Bratford, as she preferred to call him, was four years her junior. He enjoyed putting her up on this silly pedestal because he knew full well that nothing would ever come of it. He was heir to the Lievedon marquisate while she was but the daughter of the easygoing minister who was continually called in to help steer the young rakehell off the path of self-destruction.

Through an odd series of events, the Reverend Richard Kenwood had become the one moral authority on earth who seemed to have any influence over the fashionable young buck.

Lord Lievedon's prodigal son still strayed on a regular basis, but at least the scoundrel was willing to listen to Papa's wise counsel now and then. Heaven knew George's own father couldn't get through to him; but then, the grand old marquess only knew how to speak in cold, clipped commands.

At any rate, Papa's taming influence over His Lordship's firstborn was what had moved the marquess to give Papa his living. With the understanding, of course, that the Reverend Kenwood would make himself available to his patron's family whenever he was needed.

In short, when the marquess summoned them to Town, the Kenwoods went.

George tossed back the last of his brandy and signaled to a nearby footman to bring him another.

"Don't you think you've had enough?" she murmured gently.

"Just one more!" he deflected with a grin, then

hastened to change the subject. "So, my dear, how's everyone back at the village?"

The parsonage was just a stone's throw from the marquess's ancestral pile in Leicestershire.

There was always a buzz in their tiny village of Thistleton when any of His Lordship's family came down from Town. To be sure, George certainly brought his own brand of excitement out to the country. Especially last time.

"Are they all still scandalized by my little spot of mischief with the tavern wench?" Though he had the decency to look at least a little sheepish, the merry sparkle in his eyes betrayed the fact that he still thought it was funny.

Grace did not smile. "Marianne is not with child, if that's what you're asking," she answered coolly. "So at least there's that."

"Ah! What a relief."

She clenched her teeth, shocked by his nonchalance. The spoiled lordling had no idea of the harsh scrabble for existence that poor, hard-edged Marianne had left behind in London, trying, with the Kenwoods' help, to make a new life for herself in the peaceful haven of their country village.

George wasn't even aware of the damage he had so casually done to all Marianne's progress, waving more money under her nose than an ex-soiled dove could resist.

"And, er, what about Miss Windlesham?" he asked gingerly after a moment's hesitation. "Does she still hate me? As you can see, she refused the invitation to our ball tonight."

"Can you blame her?" Grace countered in surprise.

Back home, the Honorable Miss Calpurnia Windlesham was the ruling belle of the county and had all but branded George for her future husband.

He scowled. "Callie doesn't own me, you know! Nor her mother, neither," he said hotly. "Tell them I said so, Grace! Especially Lady Windlesham. That blasted woman's practically picked out the curtains already for when her daughter's the lady of Lievedon Hall."

Grace shook her head and leaned back against the wall. "I am staying out of it."

One trifled with Lady Windlesham at one's own peril.

"But Grace, you can't abandon me! You know I'm hopeless left to my own devices."

"Why don't you speak to Papa?"

"Talk to a priest about my dalliance with a demirep?" he whispered. "Hardly! What will he think of me?"

"Ex-demirep," she corrected.

"You are my only hope, Grace. You are my guiding angel—"

"Are you drunk?" she asked, merely to test his honesty.

He ignored the question. "You have to help me with Calpurnia. You fix other people's problems, Grace! Come, you know you do. That is your designated role in life and the village, and everybody knows it! Rev wouldn't be able to find his sermon notes if it weren't for you. Why, the crops would probably forget to grow if you didn't remind them, too!"

"They're not growing this year, actually, if you haven't noticed," she said dryly. "You should see my poor little garden."

The explosion of some massive volcano on the other side of the globe had robbed the earth of summer this year, and the cold was wrecking the crops. Frosts and flurries during the Season, odd-shaped hail, weird yellow skies.

Instead of the loveliness of a balmy British spring, it was gray and wet, cold and dreary.

Some people were starting to wonder if the end of the world was at hand.

The strange turn in the weather seemed all the crueler, with the war finally over. Instead of enjoying peace, now they faced the haunting specter of starvation, at least among the common folk.

There were reports of riots due to food shortages throughout England, and indeed, all of

Europe. Such hardship seemed a world away from Lord Lievedon's ballroom, but as the daughter of a pastor who also served as Overseer of the Poor for their local village, the ills of the land had become her and her father's personal problem.

Grace didn't even want to think about what corn prices were going to be like this winter. Not with all the mouths the parish had to feed.

"Well, I'm fairly sure the bloody volcano wasn't my fault, at least," George muttered.

"Language, George, please."

"Sorry."

Grace gave him a stern look but relented. "Very well. I will tell Calpurnia you asked after her."

He grabbed her hand and kissed it. "You see? You *are* an angel!" But then he continued, for he'd never been one to know when to quit. "As for Callie, well, if you want my opinion, that girl needs to learn to control her temper."

"Is that so?"

"To go into such a fury over a bit of fun with a tavern wench? Her vanity, that's the problem. Too proud! Calpurnia Windlesham thinks she is God's gift to man, but she's got bats in the belfry if she thinks she can tell *me* what to do. We're not even engaged yet!"

Grace gazed at him in calm silence while he ranted on.

"She's pretty enough, I grant you that, but the chit's ridiculously spoiled—and yes, I do see the irony of my saying so. You needn't point it out."

"Wouldn't dream of it, dear lad."

"You should warn her if she keeps this up—holding a grudge, going out of her way to try to hurt me with all her little cruel retaliations—she's going to lose her chance," he warned. "I could snap my fingers and have ten better than her by the end of the night."

"Yet here you are wasting your time talking to old, unfashionable me," Grace teased in a low tone. "What happened to all your usual admirers, anyway?"

"They've found a new idol."

"Oh, you poor, neglected thing."

"Not at all. Look at 'im, poor bleeder." George nodded across the ballroom in amusement. Following his gaze, Grace saw a crowd of women hemming in some fellow on the other side of the room. "Up to his eyeballs in matchmaking mamas—and bored Society wives on the hunt for a bit of the rough, I wager."

"George! You mustn't say such things in front of me."

He snorted. "It's the truth."

Only the top of the man's head, a shock of dark hair, could be seen above the feathered plumes adorning the ladies' jeweled coifs. "Who's that they've got cornered?"

"Lord Trevor Montgomery," George replied with a wry, knowing lift of his eyebrows. "Yes, we've got no less celebrities than the Order agents here tonight in our humble home. Are you impressed?"

Grace furrowed her brow and looked at him in question.

He saw she did not recognize the term and burst out in surprise, "Oh, by Jove's braces—my little country cousin! Don't you read the papers?"

"No. It's all too depressing. Well, enlighten me!" she exclaimed.

"Right. So it came out last month that the men we all thought were merely the depraved members of the Inferno Club were actually spies or warriors or assassins or something."

"Assassins?" she retorted, sure he was teasing her again.

"I'm deadly serious, Grace! Apparently they're part of this clandestine, hereditary order of chivalry called the Order of St. Michael the Archangel."

"You and your cock-and-bull tales."

"I'm telling you the truth!" he said, laughing merrily. "You should really open a paper now and then. They're like some remnant of the Knights

Templar or something, I swear. Handpicked for it as boys and trained for years until they're lethal, then unleashed upon the world to fight for England. You're still not impressed?"

She shrugged, eyeing him dubiously.

Even if he was not making sport of her country naïveté, she did not like violence and was not at all sure she wished to be in the same room with a government assassin.

"Apparently the Order's been around since the Crusades," he said. "They've been working for the Crown throughout the war. Bunch o' bloody heroes—"

"George, language." She sighed.

"Sorry. They were assigned all over Europe during the war, and just a month ago, they uncovered a plot right here in London to kill the Prime Minister."

"Oh, yes . . . I did hear something about that."

"I should hope so!" Then he nodded again toward the gentleman hidden by the mob of adoring females. "That chap right over there personally helped to stop the dastardly business. Once the press caught wind of it all, and the Order was exposed, the Regent saw fit to honor them in Westminster Abbey, medals and all. Ever since, the ladies won't leave poor Montgomery alone. He's one of the last bachelors left in their set. But don't bother asking him about his service. He won't discuss it—though I'm sure he has some wild tales to tell."

"Spies, you say?" she echoed skeptically, intrigued but still not quite convinced he wasn't bamming her.

"Well, ex-spies now. They can hardly do that sort of thing anymore, now that they've been lionized before the world, can they? Fame has robbed them of their vocations."

She furrowed her brow, peered again in the ex-spy's direction, but he was still hidden. She turned to George again uncertainly. "If what you say is true, are you sure they aren't dangerous?"

"Well, of course they're dangerous, but not to *us*, you little cake-head!" he said, laughing. "That's the whole point of the Crown having men like that, isn't it? From what I hear, they're trained in all types of combat and codes and ciphers, and how to make explosives." George bumped her again with his shoulder, amused at her uneasiness. "Shall I introduce you?"

"No!"

"C'mon. I'll bet he knows nine different ways to kill you with his bare hands," George declared, grinning at her alarm.

"Then perhaps those ladies should be a bit

more careful not to crowd him so," she retorted, her cheeks reddening.

He relented. "Ah, personally, I'm just glad they've found someone else to bother."

At that moment, the glittering crowd around Lord Trevor Montgomery parted, and Grace caught her first unobstructed glimpse of the visiting Order agent.

She went very still, staring in surprise. *Good heavens.* She had never seen a bona fide hero before, but Lord Trevor Montgomery certainly looked the part, dark and dashing.

He was easily over six feet tall and powerfully built, with broad shoulders that seemed to shrug off danger. He exuded virile confidence, as if there was little on earth he would not dare undertake.

He had a hard, rugged face stamped with wary cynicism that remained even when he flashed a dangerous smile at the ladies fawning on him.

At first glance, he seemed to be eating up all the attention. Though he was not a pretty fellow like some of the dandyish London peacocks strutting about tonight, he looked . . . strong.

Proud, she thought. And physically rather mighty.

She recalled what George had said about modern-day Knights Templar, and thought this man would have looked as natural in chain mail as he did in his impeccably tailored evening clothes of formal black and white.

In contrast to the gentlemanly elegance of his garb, he had long dark hair like a barbarian. Pulled back in a queue, it accented the hard angles of his square jaw and tanned skin and made him look a little, she thought, like a pirate.

Which was rather silly of her, she supposed. Odd. She was one not normally given to flights of fancy.

More distressing still were the odd tinglings in her body and daft flutterings of her heart. She dropped her gaze, startled and annoyed by her own intemperate reaction.

But unable to help herself, she stole another secret glance at him—and it was then that her gift for noticing people in pain drew her attention to the guarded, angry lines around his eyes.

The bitter intensity behind his practiced smile.

And it dawned on her that he wasn't paying the slightest bit of attention to all those women around him.

Not really.

In fact, he kept drawing away subtly from their efforts to touch him; Grace followed the line of his gaze and realized that he was constantly watching the door.

As if he was waiting for someone to arrive.

Hmm. Studying him a little more closely, she furrowed her brow and began to suspect that the "famous hero" did not want to be here any more than she did.

Of course, she might be wrong, but that smile seemed little more than a thin veneer over a vortex of churning emotion, most of it rather dark.

This was not a happy man, she mused as she gazed at him standing there like a lost soul, alone in the crowd.

George interrupted her fascinated study of the stranger as he rose. "Well, my dear Polaris, it's always a pleasure talking to you, but if you'll excuse me, I must not neglect our other guests. And . . . I believe I shall go peek in on the card games—"

"Oh George, that is not a good idea for you," she protested softly, taking his hand at once, as if she could stop him.

"Not to play! I'm only going to watch," he assured her with a smile.

Grace stared at him. "Promise?"

"If you promise to dance with me," he retorted, withdrawing his hand to fold his arms across his chest with a knowing look.

She frowned. *Stubborn pup.*

"Oh, come, one dance. I'll suffer if you will."

"Fine," she muttered, but inwardly, she shrank

from the thought of parading herself across the dance floor, a spinster in a plain, provincial gown, sporting a toe in front of the ton.

She didn't even know anyone here except for George, Papa, and, to a lesser extent, Lord Lievedon himself. It was easy to picture all these glamorous aristocrats taking one look at her, wrinkling their haughty noses, and asking each other: *"Who is* that *and what is she doing here?"*

But if that was what it took to keep George on the straight and narrow, then so be it. She'd sacrifice her dignity in front of Society if she must— and even in front of *him.* That disconcerting gentleman-assassin on the other side of the room.

Not that a man like that was ever going to notice her.

In any case, the way he watched the door made her think he was already waiting for a particular lady to arrive.

"Excellent, then!" her rakish friend declared. "I'll be back soon to claim you for our dance."

Grace nodded. *Be strong, George,* she thought, as he bowed to her, then walked away. Nevertheless, she couldn't help wishing that Callie were here.

The bubbly young belle, with her constant demand for attention, might have kept her beau distracted from his gambling habit. Then Grace could have comfortably fallen into her usual, safe role as the respectable chaperon, quietly standing behind the vivacious, golden flirt and keeping both young people in line.

She supposed she had better go check her appearance and do what she could with herself before George came back, provided his demons did not suck him down into their familiar snare.

Rising from the bench, she withdrew from the ballroom. Nobody noticed her exit.

Gliding through the marble hallways, she passed the noisy music room, full of laughter and song. Everyone here seemed to be such great friends.

She lowered her gaze and turned away, seeking a quiet room away from the crowd where she might find a mirror.

As the sounds of the ball receded, at last she peered into an empty sitting room at the end of a marble corridor.

This would suit. Stepping into the dimly lit chamber, she pulled the door closed behind her with a low sigh and finally let her guard down.

There was nothing like being a stranger in the middle of a loud, lavish party to make one feel unutterably alone.

$\mathcal{L}$ord Trevor Montgomery kept an eye on the doorway of the ballroom, but feeling more restless with every passing moment, he was starting to think that dragging himself here tonight had been a bloody waste.

Still no sign of Laura.

Faithless bitch.

Maybe she was hiding from him. Maybe she feared if she showed up here tonight, he'd start something with her new fiancé.

As if he couldn't kill one idiot dragoon with his eyes closed.

Well, she needn't have flattered herself.

He was already over Laura Bayne.

That was all that she or anyone else in London needed to know.

Hell, it wasn't as though he had been waiting the past few years to marry the feckless beauty or anything stupid like that. It wasn't as though he had been building her a bloody fucking dream house for them to live in once his service to his stupid bloody country was finally done.

But what the hell. He'd have probably hated being married to her, anyway, he told himself. He barely even knew her. He had wanted it that way, had purposely kept her at arm's length.

Still, being jilted, even by mistake, was more humiliation than he intended to stand for. So as much as he did not want to be there tonight, he had no choice.

What was left of his pride demanded he make an appearance and show the world he did not give one damn about how all his future plans had crashed and burned.

The whole ton knew how he had been written off for dead by his gorgeous fiancée while he'd been away at the war. In his own mind, Trevor had been jilted.

Thus, it was a matter of male pride. If she had had any faith in him at all, she should have known that he always came home alive. She should have believed in him.

She should have at least waited for confirmation he was dead. But she had not. She had washed her hands of him and moved on with her life.

In a way, he supposed he couldn't blame her. But he was too furious that at last, after years of faithful service, just when victory was in sight, his long-hoped-for reward had slipped through his fingers.

He felt like naught but the butt of a grand joke. Not that he was laughing.

All he knew was that there was no way in hell he would countenance anyone's pity. And so he had put on an evening coat and, he hoped, a not-too-cynical smile, and had come to show the world that he was perfectly fine.

Easy come, easy go.

All he really wanted was to be left alone, but since his horrible, newfound fame made it clear that *that* wasn't going to happen, he did the proper British thing and went about keeping up appearances.

He had come out tonight to show Laura most of all that he could move on with his life just as easily as she had.

Indeed, there were far too many women around him even now who could barely wait to comfort him in his, ahem, heartbreak.

Trevor rather hated them all at the moment.

All women. It was nothing personal. They were merely the spawn of Satan, the devil's own, every last one of 'em.

He smiled at the bloodsucking harpies, disinterested, detached, only half-listening to their idiotic prattle and wondering which of them might be any good in bed.

What pretty fools.

The three on his left were trying to get him to play a childish parlor game as their means of flirting.

"If Lord Trevor were an animal, what would he be?" they teased.

"A bear, I think," her brunette friend teased.

"Thanks a lot," he muttered.

"A wolf!"

"No, a hunting dog."

He arched a bored eyebrow.

Meanwhile, the three in the center were planning his social calendar for him. He was exhausted just listening to all the activities they were lining up for him. There was no way he was going to some stupid flower show, let alone the opera. No. He'd heard enough shrieking in Italian during that nasty business he and Nick had taken care of on the outskirts of Rome, thank you very much.

But, his eyes glazing over, he just nodded politely.

The two sultry adventuresses on his right, meanwhile, were a little more direct about what they had in mind.

Damn, they were sending him messages with their big, smoky eyes that had usually been reserved for his handsomer teammates.

But Beau was married, and Nick had gone to jail, so it seemed they were prepared to make do with boring, nice, reliable Montgomery.

He looked askance at the decadent pair, wondering if he should be worried. *Carnivores.* One licked her lips at him; the other smiled like she was thinking of tackling him to the ballroom floor and ripping his clothes off him.

There had been times in his past, of course, hundreds of miles from Laura, that he'd have been happy to comply, but this wasn't one of them.

They could all go to hell for all he cared.

Newly converted to a misanthrope, he looked away with a wave of coldness washing through him. When the clock tolled eleven, he was suddenly done with all this. This night. This petty exercise was pointless.

Obviously, Laura and the major weren't coming.

He had rather liked the notion of her walking in and seeing him surrounded by amorous women, but he had been here for two bloody hours and just didn't care that much.

She wasn't worth the aggravation.

He was going home.

It took some finesse, but he finally managed to extricate himself from the knot of rouged, vivacious lovelies. Shrugging off light, caressing holds designed to snare him; ignoring vapid questions meant to delay him; and impatiently lying through his teeth that of course he'd come back soon and dance with all of them, he retreated until he had gained his liberty, and fled.

As he marched off, he heard the ladies whispering to each other that he must be forgiven for his rudeness on account of his recent heartbreak.

Trevor gritted his teeth and strode out into the adjoining marble corridor, where more guests loitered. Out of habit, he glanced into the pier glass on the wall to check behind him and nearly paused midstride to find he was being followed.

The two little hussies in silk and diamonds did not intend to let him get away so easily, it seemed. He growled under his breath and walked faster, determined to escape them. When he picked up his pace, the whispers behind him turned to giggles, and they walked faster, too.

Did they think this was a game?

Apparently, they hadn't heard that the depraved Inferno Club had been merely a front for the Order, that its members weren't all as bad as they'd let the world believe. Especially not him.

Trevor was happy to consider himself the boring one. Responsible. Reliable. You had to be when you came from a scandalous ducal family, then were assigned for the next decade to serve on a three-man Order team with the likes of Beauchamp (flashy) and Nick bloody Forrester (bastard).

Somebody had to be the adult.

The amorous ladies hunting him obviously thought he was playing with them. He restrained the urge to turn and curtly cut them down to size.

But he couldn't have done it even if he had wanted to. Flawless manners and an inbred sense of chivalry were the bane of his existence. Like an idiot, he had even told Laura that he understood, and he had wished her happy.

What a sot.

He could hear those hussies still following him, and it wasn't difficult to guess what they desired. *Maybe I should,* he mused. Then at least he'd have the satisfaction of knowing the gossip would soon get back to Laura.

She didn't love him, but she was vain enough to be gnawed with jealousy. It was one, admittedly feeble way to get back at a woman who had publicly humiliated him.

But, no. The thought of using those harlots for his own selfish pleasure sickened him. No, he was done having sex with ulterior motives. It was bad enough to have done that sort of thing for England during his spy days. He was not about to resort to male harlotry now.

He wasn't Nick, after all.

It was time to disappear. He took a circuitous course through the marquess's excellent house to lose them. A bit of an amateur architect, he resisted the temptation to stop and study the floating spiral staircase as he passed. Adam's handiwork, no doubt.

He ducked into the music room, only to find a countess with a marriageable daughter who pinned him with a determined stare from over by the pianoforte. He'd barely extracted himself from her clutches last week.

Ah, shite. Ever so casually, Trevor pivoted and headed out the nearest door.

A nonchalant glance over his shoulder revealed Her Ladyship pushing her way through the crowd toward him.

Blazes, they were closing in on him from both directions now.

Never in his shy, pimply youth, cast in the shadow of his better-looking, louder-bragging friends had he ever dreamed he might have this sort of problem.

He headed for a nearby servant door, but a stream of footmen spilled out, cutting him off; trapped, he glanced about, seeking another escape, then slipped around the corner and sped down the hall. He could hear the pursuing ladies just around the corner.

"Oh, Lord Trevor, darling, where are you?"

"We want to ask you something, handsome!"

He scowled.

"Yoo-hoo? Where have you gone, my lord?"

"We have a wonderful notion of how to cheer you up!"

Their giggling grew louder.

"Perdition," he whispered under his breath. Laying hold of the nearest doorknob, he whisked into a dimly lit parlor, pulled the door shut silently behind him, and locked it. Immediately touching his fingertips to his tongue, he reached over and pinched out the flames on the nearby candle sconce.

Then he held perfectly still in the darkness, waiting for them to pass.

He held his breath as the ladies tried the door.

"No, Cecily, this one's locked."

"Come, he must've gone upstairs."

"Oooh! Yes! What a wicked tease! Maybe he's already found a bed for us . . ."

He rolled his eyes, but finally, he heard them moving off. He let out a weary exhalation and leaned his forehead against the door. *That was close.*

"Um, excuse me," a feminine voice spoke up from the darkness.

Trevor nearly jumped out of his skin. *Not another one!* He whirled around, taken more off guard than any ex-spy should ever be and irked in the extreme by that fact.

It just went to show how out of sorts he still was over, well, everything these days.

But as he focused on an hourglass figure silhouetted in the moonlight streaming through the French doors to the little balcony, he could not believe his eyes.

You have got to be joking, he thought. Another blasted woman waiting for him?

What the hell?

His eyes narrowed. *Is that what these wenches think of me? That they can do whatever they want with me? Take advantage of me? Use me?*

Well, then. Maybe Nick was right. He had always warned Trevor about being too nice to people. This was what nice, respectable gentlemen got: walked on.

No more, he vowed, suddenly full-on furious at this ambush and fed up with these games.

How this little predatory female had known to lie in wait for him here, he was too outraged to wonder. He truly could not be bothered to care.

Pushed past the point of chivalry, he decided it was bloody well time to fight fire with fire. Teach these huntresses a lesson they'd never forget. He didn't know which one had trapped him this time, but she was about to get more than she had bargained for.

"Well, my dear," he purred, stalking slowly toward the shapely outline of the woman. "Here we are," he said coldly. "Alone at last."

"What? Oh—I—um—I'm sorry—I—"

"Don't lose your nerve now, *chérie*," he taunted her in a low, silken voice. "You've got me all to yourself. I'm at your service, I assure you. Such persistence deserves to be rewarded." He moved closer. "I'm here to give you what you want. So let's get started, shall we?"

*G*race stood there tongue-tied as Lord Trevor Montgomery stepped out of the shadows, looming before her like a mighty fallen angel with merciless hatred in his eyes. There was not even time to scream as he swept her roughly into his arms; he clamped her against his iron chest and claimed her mouth in an angry, insolent kiss.

Lord Lovedon's Duel

LORETTA CHASE

"*We*'d best do it now," Chloe Sharp told her older sister. "Say goodbye and bawl, so that we don't make a spectacle of ourselves, or set Mama off."

"Y-yes. Oh, Chloe, I'll miss you so!" Althea fell weeping on Chloe's neck, heedless of the wrinkles and stains she made on two of London's costliest dresses.

Bride and bridesmaid stood in a dimly lit passage that ran between the picture gallery, which extended the west wing's full length, and the smaller of the two drawing rooms. The larger, the Gold Drawing Room, occupied the center of the first floor of the Duke of Marchmont's Jacobean mansion. There hundreds of wedding guests were celebrating Althea's marriage to Prince Louis of Massbeck-Holveg. From the passage, though, the merriment was practically inaudible.

This was the last time Chloe would see her sister for a long time. Her heart was breaking. Still, she made herself draw away.

"That's enough," she said. "We don't want the Beau Monde to see us with tear-streaked faces and crushed bows and creases. Come out into the gallery, where we'll have some light, and I can put you back to rights."

She started to open the door to the gallery, but paused as a wave of masculine laughter spilled toward them. Althea stopped, too, and caught hold of Chloe's arm. They both giggled the way they used to do when they were children, hiding to spy on grown-ups.

"But everybody knows he was obliged to give up the girl he loved," somebody said. Mr. Crawford? Chloe had met so many aristocrats today that their names and faces were a hopeless muddle in her brain.

"Which girl was that?" another man said.

"A sweetheart Prince Louis left behind in Massbeck-Holveg," Crawford said. "Lovers torn asunder, you know, by Fate."

Althea inhaled sharply, her grip on Chloe's arm tightening.

"Love, gentlemen, is a luxury His Highness cannot afford," said a deep, drawling voice. "Three royal castles in his speck of a country, and all of them falling to pieces. He doesn't need love: He needs new chimneys."

Though Chloe had never heard that voice before today, she knew who it belonged to: James Bransby, the Earl of Lovedon.

A leader of fashion, one of Prince Louis's dearest English friends, a favorite of the King and Queen, and famously whimsical, he was London's most elusive bachelor.

The men went off again, into whoops this time, as though it was the wittiest thing they'd ever heard.

"Come away," Chloe whispered to her sister. "There's a doorway to another room—"

"He's hardly the first of the King's cousins to come to England for a rich wife," Lovedon continued. "For them, this sort of thing is merely a business transaction. Naturally he'll put aside any personal disappointments with Teutonic fortitude, like the staunch patriot he is."

While he spoke, Chloe was aware of Althea's breath coming faster and faster. She gave a small, choked cry, and let go of Chloe's arm.

Though she wanted to push Lord Lovedon out of a window, Chloe had to tend to her sister first. She pulled Althea toward another doorway, an open one leading to one of the back staircases. Althea was sobbing again, this time in deep, painful gulps.

Chloe half-dragged her to the door on the other side of the landing, through the recently abandoned dining room, and into a pretty sitting room. Its lone window overlooked the splendid gardens that spread out for miles, it seemed, from the north front of the house. Thanks to the afternoon's onslaught of rain, a grey haze shrouded the glorious vista Chloe had glimpsed this morning.

She grasped Althea by the upper arms and gently shook her. "Those men are *drunk*," she said. She was none too sober herself, she realized, as a wave of dizziness nearly toppled her. Firmly ignoring it, she went on bracingly, "I was amazed to see how much champagne Lord Lovedon could pour down his throat and still stand upright. But you know what aristocrats are like: heads of oak, and hearts even harder."

"It—it wasn't a secret. Prince Louis told me he was poor—but he s-said he l-loved me."

"Which he does, as everyone can see—except Lord Lovedon and his dimwitted followers. But you can't expect them to recognize a love match when they see one. Defective vision, you know, thanks to centuries of inbreeding—and the pox, too, probably. And don't forget the gallons of champagne they've swilled, or the fact that they do nothing but gossip because they lack the mental capacity to carry on an intelligent conversation. My love, you can't possibly take them seriously."

"But what if it's true?" Althea said. "Only think of Prince Louis pining for the girl he loves, while having to pretend to care for me."

"If there was such a girl, he forgot her the instant he clapped eyes on you," Chloe said. "I was there, recollect, on the day His Highness came into Maison Noirot with Lord Longmore."

Mama had patronized the French dressmakers practically from the day they opened their shop. Chloe and Althea had been waiting in the showroom for her when Prince Louis and the Earl of Longmore entered.

"Once His Highness got his first look at you, he couldn't see or think about anything else," Chloe said. "He certainly didn't know then that you were rich."

"H-he could have g-guessed, I wasn't p-poor," Althea said, "considering it's the most expensive dressmaking shop in L-London."

Chloe dismissed this with a wave. "The point is, he fell over head and ears in love with you, and everybody knows it except this pack of drunken degenerates. How can you let a lot of strutting ignoramus blockheads make you wretched on your wedding day?"

She went on in this way while she swiftly set about repairing the outward damage. Combining relentless mockery and mimicry of Lord Lovedon & Company with more practical remedies—the careful application of a handkerchief, readjustment of hairpins, and smoothing of wrinkles—she soon restored Althea to the state of glowing happiness she'd enjoyed only a short time earlier. By the time Althea returned to her prince—who lit up, by the way, at the sight of her—she was giggling.

Bride and bridegroom disappeared into the mob of well-wishers.

Chloe looked about her. All was in hand.

Except for one small detail.

She took a glass of champagne from a tray a passing footman presented to her, swallowed the contents, set the empty glass down on the nearest horizontal surface, then started back the way she'd come.

This time when Chloe opened the door to the picture gallery, the male laughter sounded farther away.

As she entered, she saw them gathered at the great bay window overlooking the north front.

He was easy enough to spot.

The Earl of Lovedon was tall and dark, yes, but not handsome. His features were too harsh and angular for classical beauty . . . although from the neck down he was all too classical, like a Greek statue. That chiseled profile and athletic physique had claimed her attention all too often this day. The view had left her much too warm and breathing too fast.

His big shoulders propping up a corner of the window embrasure, the usual faint, superior smile curving his cynical mouth, he stood with arms folded, one long leg crossed in front of the other. The casual stance displayed the highest level of tailor's art: His fine wool coat skimmed the contours of his broad shoulders and chest, and his black trousers hugged his muscular legs.

If he hadn't had something to lean on, he'd probably fall on his face, the drunken moron.

The men were too busy gossiping and laughing to notice her approach until she was practically under their noses.

Then Lord Lovedon's dark gaze slanted her way.

"Ah, Miss Sharp," he said lazily. "Taken a wrong turn, have you? The duke's house is something of a labyrinth. All sorts of odd corners and not-so-secret floors between floors. Happily, you needn't fear his mad aunt's springing out of a concealed door. She's moved to Torquay."

Chloe stripped off one of her gloves and struck his cheek with it. She grabbed a glass of champagne from one of his startled companions and threw the contents in his face.

He didn't so much as flinch. The champagne dripped from his face onto his perfect neck cloth and down over his splendid silk waistcoat.

Over the room's sudden silence, the rain's hammering sounded like drumbeats. Her heart beat a harder and faster tempo.

"What is *wrong* with you?" she said. "How could you say such *hurtful* things? At a *wedding*, no less! How dare you make my sister cry on her wedding day, of all days? You *brute*."

"I say," someone said.

"What the devil?" someone else said.

She ignored them. "If I were a man," she said, "I'd draw your cork for you. I'd— No. Why do I need to be a man? Be so good as to name your second, my lord."

She was aware of hurried footsteps behind her, and familiar voices. Her sister Sarah had come. And Amy Renfrew, Chloe's dearest friend after Althea.

"Oh, Lord, I knew it," Sarah said. "I saw that look. I know that look."

"Come away, Chloe," Amy said. "Whatever it is, let it be."

"Name your second, Lord Lovedon," Chloe said.

"Second?" Amy said.

Someone laughed.

"I believe Miss Sharp has challenged Lord Lovedon to a . . . duel?" one of the men said.

Chloe didn't know or care who spoke or who laughed. The world was a red fog of rage, and she could barely see. Except for him. His lordly hulk was all too clear, and she wanted to choke him, this spoiled lout who'd upset her sweet, gentle sister on what was supposed to be the happiest day of her life.

He stood, eyebrows aloft, still smiling his superior little smile. A drop of champagne clung to his thick black eyelashes. Another drop trickled down the hard angle of his jaw into his snow-white neck cloth.

"Oh, no," Sarah said. She grabbed Chloe's arm and tried to drag her away. "You can*not* make a scene, Chloe. Not here. Not *now*."

"A scene," Chloe said, her gaze locked with Lovedon's glittering black one. "I'll make a scene. By Jupiter, I'll—"

"Come away, Chloe," Amy said, taking hold of the other arm. "Whatever the trouble is, this is not the time."

"For God's sake, come away," Sarah said.

"I recommend you heed the ladies' advice, Miss Sharp," Lord Lovedon said. "Under no circumstances could I possibly agree to meet a young lady at thirty paces." He took out a large linen handkerchief, embroidered with an *L*, and calmly wiped his face. "I should be a deuced laughingstock."

"Yet it doesn't trouble you to make a laughingstock of one who has done you no injury," she said. "It's quite all right to demean someone you know nothing about—"

"Chloe, let it be," Amy whispered. "Come away before any of the others come looking for you."

Chloe wasn't done. She wanted to hurt him, the way he'd hurt Althea. But he was unreachable, the aloof, immovable aristocrat. He still wore the mocking little smile. He remained perfectly cool and collected even while he wiped his face.

Meanwhile her hands were shaking, and it took all the willpower she had to keep her voice at an even pitch.

"I shall expect to hear from your friends tomorrow morning," she said. "Or I shall evermore regard you as no gentleman—and a coward as well."

She shook off her sister and friend, turned on her heel, and walked away.

$\mathscr{L}$ovedon watched her go.

The two girls fluttered anxiously about her. Miss Sharp didn't flutter. She didn't hurry away, either, which was generous of her. She had some fifty feet to travel to the door she must have irrupted from. This gave him ample time to appreciate the rear view.

For an inebriated female of negligible rank, she carried herself surprisingly well, tall and straight, without seeming stiff in the least. The only sign of unsteadiness was the slight undulation of her hips. The motion made her long, lacy scarf dance about her, and set the bows and ruffles of her pink dress atremble.

Until this moment, Miss Sharp had been no more to him than one of the numerous sisters and cousins and friends of the bride garbed in gorgeously extravagant dresses. He'd been introduced to them all, and his fearsome memory retained every name.

Beyond being able to put a name to her face— and catching Miss Sharp putting her gloved hand to her eye once or twice during the nuptials—he'd given her little thought. The girls were young and, for the most part, unsophisticated. The rites were lengthy and stupendously boring, and the fête thereafter, likewise in the tradition of the bridegroom's forbears, featured his country's quaint music. The music had driven Lovedon from the Gold Drawing Room to the picture gallery.

As one of the groom's attendants, he couldn't flee the house. His early departure would be taken a slight, and even he knew better than to offend one of the King's favorite cousins. Having no choice, Lovedon had remained, bored and irritated to within a hairsbreadth of insanity. He'd drunk enough champagne to float a flagship—possibly the entire Royal Navy—to no discernible effect.

Until a moment ago.

The last dose, the one Miss Sharp had administered externally, had brightened his mood amazingly. The eyes flashing at him had turned out be an interesting shade of green, with gold flecks. Her hair, which he'd previously dismissed as an insipid light brown, turned out to be the color of honey. Her skin was flawless, and the angry pink tingeing her cheeks had turned ordinary prettiness into something almost beautiful. Most important, she'd turned out to have a *personality*.

He watched until she'd turned into the doorway halfway down the gallery.

"Well, that was cool and refreshing," he said as he folded his handkerchief.

"What the devil was that about?" Hempton said.

"No idea," Lovedon said. He put the handkerchief away.

"Do you think she was foxed?" Crawford said.

Beyond a doubt. Though Lovedon hadn't thought he'd paid her any particular attention, his memory held images of Miss Sharp taking one after another glass of champagne from the many trays making their way through the crowd in the Gold Drawing Room.

Now he wondered what she was trying to drown.

Not boredom, surely, in her case. After all, it wasn't every day that a lawyer's daughter married a prince, and her sisters and friends enjoyed the privilege of mingling with the haut ton. Perhaps Miss Sharp had simply celebrated to excess her sister's matrimonial triumph. Or perhaps she wasn't used to superior champagne.

"I shouldn't venture to say," he said. "Women get emotional at weddings. She became overwrought."

"And abandoned the festivities, journeyed through two rooms and a passage where everybody takes a wrong turn and gets lost for days, then down half the length of the picture gallery—all to take it out on you?" Bates said.

"It's possible I said the wrong thing," Lovedon said.

"I should say that's more than likely," Bates said. "I'd better smooth the ruffled feathers before any Highnesses or Majesties get wind of it."

Lovedon abruptly recollected that the lady, being the bride's sister, was the Prince of Massbeck-Holveg's sister-in-law. A short time earlier, Lovedon had expressed certain less-than-sentimental views of the match. Prince Louis would not find those comments amusing.

If any unpleasantness resulted from Lovedon's little contretemps with Miss Sharp, he would receive a royal summons, a royal dressing-down (a skill at which the King, a former naval commander, excelled), and orders to make groveling apologies to about a thousand people, mostly foreigners.

"I ought to do that," Lovedon said. He started to push himself away from the wall.

Bates held up a hand. "You've done enough damage. I've never before seen you deal so clumsily with a woman. You'd do well to leave this to me."

*I*nsisting that she needed to calm down before she returned to the company, Amy and Sarah steered Chloe into the sitting room where she'd revived her sister's spirits.

Sarah commenced by berating her.

That was so calming.

"A lord!" Sarah cried. "And *that* one, of all lords! What on earth possessed you? He looked wet. You threw a drink at him, didn't you? Oh, Chloe, tell me you didn't."

"It seems she did," Amy said. "And challenged him to a duel as well."

"I thought of stabbing him with one of the carving knives," Chloe said, "but the servants had taken them all back to the kitchen."

"Oh, Chloe!" Sarah cried.

"What on earth did he do?" Amy said.

The blind rage was abating, and a conglomeration of feelings were sweeping in, including a sorrow Chloe was afraid would overwhelm her.

"I took exception to something he said," Chloe said. "Would you be so kind as to take Sarah back to the party? I need a moment's peace and quiet to collect myself, and I can't do that while she's taking fits."

"I am not taking fits! And you're a fine one to talk!"

Amy took Sarah's arm. "My dear, we're all agitated. What's a wedding without some hysteria? But Chloe's right. She needs time to compose herself, and our making a fuss isn't helpful."

She led Sarah away, but slowed once to look over her shoulder and mouth, "Later."

Chloe had hardly a minute's solitude before she heard footsteps, followed swiftly by a male voice. "Ah, there you are, Miss Sharp."

She didn't have to look that way to know it wasn't *his* voice.

She was on the brink of tears again—what a ninny she was, to regret her sister's happiness and fret about brainless aristocrats!—but she blinked hard and lifted her chin.

The gentleman—she couldn't remember his name—smiled as he approached. "Miss Sharp, I shall not waste words," he said. "I've come to beg your pardon for any offense Lord Lovedon has caused."

"Has he appointed you his second?" she said.

He gave a nervous laugh. "No, no, certainly not."

"Then why send a proxy?" she said. "Why not make his own apology?"

"He didn't send me," the gentleman said. "He's a bit . . ." He trailed off, frowning, apparently at a loss for the right word.

"A bit of an ass," she said.

"Bates thinks I'm half-seas over and not to be trusted with delicate diplomatic negotiations, Miss Sharp," came another, deeper voice, from the doorway.

No doubt whose drawling baritone that was.

Mr. Bates said something under his breath. Curses, Chloe supposed. She was tempted to utter several unladylike words herself. She wasn't nearly ready for another confrontation.

Though her heart beat so hard she thought she'd faint, she collected what remained of her dignity and made herself regard Lord Lovedon as coolly as he'd regarded her moments ago.

He didn't stagger into the room. He had too much self-control for that . . . even though they seemed to be upon a ship at sea.

The walls and floor ought not to be moving.

She'd been too furious before to notice but . . . maybe she oughtn't to have taken that last glass of champagne.

She forced herself to meet his mocking black gaze. "You needn't be anxious, Lord Lovedon," she said. "I shan't create an international incident. I never tattle, and Althea is unforgivably forgiving. To calm her, I told her you were spouting nonsense because you were drunk as well as not very intelligent. By now, I daresay, she's not only forgiven you but has even made up a reason to think kindly of you. My sister—as Prince Louis had the *discernment* to recognize—is angelically beautiful not only outwardly but inwardly as well. She's incapable of thinking unkindly of anybody. She'd make excuses for Satan himself."

He drew nearer, blocking her view of his friend—and everything else. He loomed over her, all dark wool and blinding white linen and a gloriously embroidered—and now damp—blue silk waistcoat that must have cost as much as her dress.

"Am I to understand that you came and challenged me to a duel and made me quake in my boots—all for nothing?" he said.

"*She* has forgiven you," Chloe said. "I am not so saintly. I have not. You haven't apologized."

Nor would he, she supposed. Some men would rather be roasted on a spit and fed to wild boars than apologize, especially to a woman.

"It seems I must kill myself," he said. "It is impossible to continue in this world without Miss Sharp's approbation." He put the back of his hand to his forehead. "Farewell, all. I go to a better place."

"I think not," she said. "I think it will be rather worse than this one and a good deal hotter."

"But all my friends will join me there eventually," he said. "I shall hope in time to see you there as well. You did say you weren't saintly."

"In that case," she said, "I wish you a very long, unceasingly unhappy life."

She gave him an exaggerated version of the simpering smile so many other women wasted on him, and dipped a little curtsey . . . and then kept sinking.

*L*ovedon lunged and caught her up in his arms before she toppled.

This wasn't the simplest feat. He wasn't as steady on his legs as he'd supposed, and she, with her great ballooning sleeves and billowing skirts, wasn't easy to capture securely.

Then, once he had her, he wasn't sure what to do with her. He thought of carrying her home and putting her to bed. He thought that might be fun.

Miss Renfrew hurried in. "Chloe, they're leav—" She stopped short.

"Miss Sharp is not well," Bates said.

"Excess of . . . excitement," Lovedon said.

"We need to revive her," Bates said.

"She needs to go to bed . . . and sleep it off," Lovedon said. She was flushed, and under the miles of silk there seemed to be a splendidly rounded body, invitingly warm. His head dipped a little, and he inhaled a delicious blend of scents: soap and flowers and Woman.

She stirred in his arms. "Put me down."

"Probably not wise," he said, "considering you can't stand up."

"I need to say goodbye to the *happy* couple,"

she said. Her voice was slurred. "The madly-in-love-with-each-other couple."

"If you try to walk unaided, you'll fall on your face," Lovedon told her.

"If you keep trying to carry me, you'll fall on *your* face," she said. "I'll lean on Amy. Please put me down and go away. To the devil, preferably."

She was shapely and highly entertaining and she smelled delectable. Lovedon wanted to take her to a private corner—the house abounded in secret nooks and crannies—and set about winning her over. In her present condition, though, that would be unsporting. In any case, he preferred a woman to be fully conscious when he set about seducing her.

He let her down very carefully, so carefully that he felt every inch of her descent. For one heady moment, her breasts pressed against his chest. When her feet touched the floor, he cautiously released her. She started to turn away, swayed, and grabbed his lapels.

His arm went around her neat little waist.

"Oh, Lord," she said. "I do believe I'm actually drunk."

"You can't be drunk *now*," Miss Renfrew said. "It's time to take leave of the newlyweds."

"I . . . don't . . . know," Miss Sharp said. "I really need . . . to sit . . . lie . . . down." She slumped against Lovedon. "You smell like starch," she said. "And something else."

"Listen to me," he said. "You can do this, Miss Sharp. If you don't, your sister will wonder what's wrong. You don't want to worry her, I know."

"You were mean to her." She looked up at him, green-gold eyes wide and accusing and slightly crossed.

"Yes, I'm a brute," he said. "Ten minutes. That's all we'll need. I'll give you my arm and Miss Renfrew will support you discreetly on the other side. And Bates will bring up the rear. The crush will be so great that no one will notice we're propping you up. You'll wish the couple well and make your curtseys—"

"If I curtsey, I don't think I'll be able to get up again. I think I'd like to lie on the floor, please."

"Ten minutes," he said. "Pretend to be perfectly well for ten minutes, that's all. Then we'll get you safely away. If you'll do this, you and I shall have our duel."

She blinked up at him. "I get to shoot you?"

"Yes."

She smiled, and it was the genuine article this time. Her mouth softened and curved and her face took on the kind of blissful expression a man was accustomed to see—if he was skillful—in more intimate situations. His lower regions, which didn't understand the concept of proper time and place, became primed for action. And his mood soared so high so swiftly that his head spun, and the room whirled along with it.

The rain continued to beat at the windows, but in his world the sun had broken out, and life had blossomed into riotous colors.

"Very well," she said. "I accept your terms."

*G*etting Miss Sharp through those ten minutes wasn't the easiest thing Lovedon had ever done, though it might have been the most amusing. He suspected he'd damaged an internal organ, keeping a straight face throughout the proceedings.

But with Bates's and Miss Renfrew's help, he got her through the goodbyes. There followed several other interesting maneuvers, including flat-out lying to her parents while Miss Renfrew guarded her in an antechamber.

The crowd, the heat, fatigue, combined with strong emotion, had proved too much for Miss Sharp, Lovedon told them. To avoid disrupting the family's remaining commitments for the day, he offered to send her home in his carriage with her friend, Miss Renfrew.

Though initially alarmed, they did not, in fact, have much attention to spare their eldest unwed daughter. He knew they had other engagements this day, including a reception at Windsor, because he was expected to appear at the same events. After only a few mild protests about his lordship's taking so much trouble, they consented.

That done, Lovedon smuggled the drunken bridesmaid down the steep back staircase in the west wing to the ground floor. With him clasping her arm, she was able to get down the narrow stairs more or less unaided. As soon as they came out under the south front's arcade, though, the fresh air hit her—or rather she hit it, much in the way one runs abruptly into a wall.

She tottered backward. He caught hold of her, then wrapped one arm about her shoulder. "Now, *stay*," he said.

She heaved a great sigh and leaned against him. The top of her head came to his chin. They stood in the shelter of the great arcade, out of sight of anybody happening to look out of the windows. It was a fine opportunity to get up to no good . . . but she wasn't in proper condition. Not to mention that Bates stood only a few paces away, having a terse whispered dispute with Miss Renfrew.

Lovedon stood stoically with his armful of drunken deliciousness and gazed down the driveway, watching his carriage approach through the rain.

"Don't forget," came a slurred voice from the environs of his neck cloth.

He looked down.

She gazed somberly up at him.

"Believe me, I shall not forget this day," he said.

"Our duel," she said. "It was good of you to stop me from falling down, but . . ." She stared at him for a long moment.

"Think nothing of it, Miss Sharp," he said. "It's hardly the first time I've helped a drunken friend home."

She wagged a gloved finger under his chin. "Ah, but I'm not your friend."

"That's what you think," he said.

"I'll never be your friend," she said. "Though I will admit . . ." She bit her lower lip. A tiny crease appeared between her delicately arched eyebrows.

She was thinking, obviously.

He pictured thoughts staggering through her brain, trying to find their way.

The carriage neared, and Bates stepped out under one of the arcade's arches to signal the coachman where to stop. A footman leapt off the back, opened an umbrella, and hurried toward them.

After seeing Miss Renfrew stowed safely inside, the footman returned. Keeping a firm hold of Miss Sharp, Lovedon steered her toward the vehicle.

Getting her into it wanted ingenuity and quick reflexes. He could only hope that his broad back in combination with the large umbrella and the rain would prevent any onlookers in the house from observing the performance.

When he'd finally got her foot securely on the carriage step, she said, "I'll admit I might have made a small error of judgment."

"You made a fatal error," he said. "You attracted my attention. Now you'll have the devil of a time getting rid of me." He gave her a push. Miss Renfrew quickly reached out and pulled her friend, who landed on the seat in a flurry of swishing silk. She laughed. "Oh, you silly man."

The footman closed the door and Lovedon backed away from the carriage.

A moment later, the vehicle rolled away. He watched it go. As it reached the first curve of the driveway, the window went down and a white-gloved hand appeared and gave a jaunty wave.

Lovedon House
18th June, half-past eleven o'clock

Madam:
I shall expect to meet you at dusk this day at Battersea Fields for the purpose of defending my honor against the charges of being a coward and no

gentleman. I shall supply the weapons, and Bates will act as my friend, whether he likes it or not.

A ticket porter has been engaged to loiter in the vicinity of your home. A written reply given into his keeping will make its way both discreetly and speedily to me.

I have the honor to be,

Madam,

Your obedient servant,

Lovedon

Portman Square
18th June, one o'clock

My Lord:

I have the honor to acknowledge the receipt of your lordship's letter, which is thoroughly ridiculous. If your lordship thinks I propose to be hanged for killing a peer—and I ought to point out that I am an excellent shot—I recommend your lordship think again. Yesterday, as your lordship is well aware, I was deep in my cups—and it is perfectly beastly of your lordship to remind me of the fact.

I have the honor to be,

My Lord,

Your lordship's obedient servant,

Chloe Sharp

Lovedon House
18th June, half-past two o'clock

Madam:

    I have the honor to acknowledge the receipt
of your letter of one o'clock. Does this mean you
retract your words and apologize?

    I have the honor to be,
    Madam,
    Your obedient servant,
      Lovedon

Portman Square
18th June, three o'clock

My Lord:

    I would rather hang than apologize to you. For
anything. Ever.

    I have the honor to be,
    My Lord,
    Your lordship's obedient servant,
      Chloe Sharp

Lovedon House
18th June, half-past three o'clock

Madam:

    Your having declined to give the reparation

which I consider myself entitled to receive, I now call upon you to give me that satisfaction for your conduct which a gentleman has a right to require, and which a gentleman never refuses to give. I shall expect to see you at Battersea Fields at seven o'clock this evening.

> *I have the honor to be,*
> *Madam,*
> *Your obedient servant,*
> > *Lovedon*

P.S. I dare you.

Portman Square
18th June, half-past four o'clock

My Lord:
The satisfaction which your lordship has demanded, it is of course impossible for me to decline.

> *I have the honor to be,*
> *My Lord,*
> *Your lordship's obedient servant,*
> > *Chloe Sharp*

Battersea Fields, half-past seven o'clock

*C*hloe stood by the cabriolet in which she and Amy had arrived. The setting sun cast a golden glow over the marshy wasteland, and she was pretending to be perfectly calm, enjoying the scenery, while Amy and Mr. Bates carried on their fussing about various dueling rules.

Lord Lovedon stood no great distance away, by his carriage—the one that had taken her home last night.

Her face didn't go up in flames at the recollection because it didn't need to. Her face had been burning since this morning, when the ferocious pounding behind her eyes had begun to abate enough to allow her memory to take over the job of tormenting her.

She had remembered, then, every single thing that had happened yesterday afternoon, down to the moment when she'd sent Lord Lovedon a saucy wave from his carriage window.

She'd discovered this morning what it meant to die of embarrassment.

A reasonable man of even minimal sensibility would have realized that she'd suffered enough for her extremely stupid and unladylike behavior.

A man of delicacy and understanding would

have the tact to leave her to squirm with shame in the privacy of her home.

But no. He had to rub her face in it.

And now she had this idiot duel to fight, when they both knew that neither of them would do anything but fire into the air.

He probably thought it was amusing.

Everyone said he was whimsical.

Good grief, would Amy and Mr. Bates never cease bickering?

"They're making quite a project of this," came a deep, drawling voice from somewhere above her shoulder.

She gave a start and a mortifying little squeak of surprise.

"Was it absolutely necessary to sneak up on me?" she said.

"I'm over six feet tall in my bare feet," he said. "I'm wearing boots and a hat—and while I'll admit my clothes are uniformly dark, as is de rigueur for a duel, I should have thought I was hard to miss, Miss Sharp."

"I was not paying attention," she said. "I was . . . thinking."

"I observed that you were not paying attention to me," he said. "That's why I brought myself closer."

She remembered being swept up in his arms.

She remembered the feel of his hand at the back of her waist, keeping her steady. She remembered his arm about her shoulders . . . the warmth and strength of his big body.

The sun was sinking but it seemed to be blazing down on her, on everything, and all the world seemed to be softening and melting.

She didn't want to melt. She didn't want to be one of the scores of women waiting for the exclusive attention he was probably incapable of giving.

Still, she remembered what he'd said yesterday and the way he'd charmed her by degrees without her quite realizing. She recalled the series of witty, provoking notes he'd sent this day . . . and how she'd wished he'd come in person to annoy her, so that she could throw something at him—and at the same time she'd laughed, too, at his absurd messages. And she had very greatly enjoyed composing her answers.

"Amy has never acted as a second before, and she spent two hours studying Papa's copy of *The British Code of Duel*," she said. "It's her fault we weren't exactly on time—because she insisted that we couldn't proceed without a surgeon in attendance. I told her that was silly. If I kill you, no surgeon can do you any good. If I only wound you, naturally I shall leave you to bleed to death."

"I'm sure that goes without saying," he said in a stifled voice.

She looked up sharply. His expression was far too innocent.

"I know you think this is a hilarious joke, taunting me to come out to this place," she said.

"I wasn't sure how else to get you alone," he said.

"We are not alone," she said.

He glanced toward Amy and Mr. Bates, who seemed to having a controversy about the weapons. "This will do. For the moment."

"Since we are somewhat alone," she said, "I ought to warn you: I've actually decided not to kill you, no matter how great the temptation. I shall fire into the air."

"I beg you will not," he said. "You might harm an innocent bird."

"I most certainly will not fire at you."

"It would only be fair," he said. "Because I most certainly mean to fire at you."

"No, you don't," she said.

"I do—and I urge you to shoot straight at me," he said. "I promise you'll feel better afterward. *Trust me.*"

Amy stomped toward them. "This is most irregular," she said. "The combatants are not supposed to be enjoying a tête-à-tête."

"Lord Lovedon was bored," Chloe said. "He came to amuse himself at my expense, because you and Mr. Bates are taking an eternity."

"What seems to be the difficulty?" Lord Lovedon said.

"The dueling ground," Amy said.

"Ah, yes," Lord Lovedon said. "According to *The British Code of Duel*, as Miss Renfrew is now aware, the seconds must 'choose out a snug sequestered spot, where the ground is level, and no natural, terrestrial, or celestial line presenting itself to assist either party in his views of sending his opponent into eternity.'"

Chloe stared at him.

"I have a terrifying memory," Lord Lovedon said.

"Well, we've settled it," Amy said. "Lord Lovedon, would you be so good as to accompany Mr. Bates. Chloe, you're to come with me."

*T*he seconds chose the place where the Duke of Wellington and the Earl of Winchilsea had fought their duel a few years ago. It was the site Lovedon had suggested to Bates—fitting, Lovedon thought, today being the twentieth anniversary of Waterloo. Though Miss Renfrew evidently required persuading, she had to see it was a suitable spot, a stretch of flat ground near the river, not easily visible to passersby.

One had to cross a drainage ditch to get there. Lovedon offered to carry Miss Sharp over it.

"That won't be necessary," she told him. "Today I'm painfully sober."

He watched her make the small leap. For a second, her skirts lifted, and he had a glimpse of purple half-boots. He smiled.

It was the one bright element in her attire. She'd worn what he guessed was an archery dress: The dark blue garment's sleeves were not the vast, ballooning ones fashion dictated, but fitted tight, especially along the lower arms. Instead of an immense bonnet festooned with feathers and ribbons and lace, she wore a tiny black hat.

The costume made her a narrower target.

He supposed she'd done it on purpose to mock him. That was more or less why he'd donned dueling dress: uniformly dark clothing, including his neck cloth, which was black. He was mocking himself, as well he ought.

Thanks to boredom and drink, he'd been a stupendous lout yesterday. Yet if he'd behaved well, he wouldn't have discovered her. He wouldn't have had the fun of writing incendiary notes and picturing her gleefully composing her replies.

He watched the seconds gravely mark out the

field. Then Miss Renfrew guided Miss Sharp to her place. Bates, wearing a look of exasperation, approached and said, "You'll stand here—and you had better pray that nobody gets wind of this."

"My lips are sealed," Lovedon said.

"How I wish that were ever true," Bates said.

He then proceeded to the halfway point between the duelists and asked if there was any possibility of reconciliation.

Miss Sharp shook her head.

Bates looked to Lovedon.

He shook his head.

The lowering sun gilded the fields. A gentle breeze caressed his face.

What a splendid evening for a duel, he thought.

*T*rust me.

Amy put the pistol in Chloe's hand. It was quite small and oddly shaped, double-barreled, and stunningly ornate: gold, with exquisite enameling, and set with pearls and diamonds. She stared at it.

"It's French," Amy said. "You cock it with this." She indicated a part. "Then it works the same as any other pistol, Mr. Bates said. But it has a very short range. I suspect it's easier to injure somebody by hitting them in the head with the grip.

In any event, we need to shorten the dueling distance. Do you mind? I pointed out to Mr. Bates that the minimum distance is no less than three yards. I do wish I knew what was in Lord Lovedon's mind."

"He's whimsical," Chloe said.

"Yes, everyone says so. And it's mere form, of course. So many duels are, you know. One goes through the motions—"

"Yes, yes," Chloe broke in impatiently. "But we must do it Lord Lovedon's way." She'd called him a coward and no gentleman. She'd refused to apologize. That, Amy had said, gave him the choice of weapons and terms. And the first shot. "If he wants to dirty his pretty French pistols by shooting them off, that's his choice."

Shoot straight at me . . . Trust me.

Though she knew—she was *positive*—she had nothing to be afraid of, her heart was pounding very hard. She cocked the weapon as Amy had instructed and held it down by her side.

She was aware of Lord Lovedon following the same procedure, but it was a distant awareness. So many wild thoughts raced through her mind that she couldn't keep up with them, let alone make sense of them. Her heart wouldn't slow. She knew nothing terrible would happen, yet she was panicking all the same.

She was aware of Lord Lovedon coming much closer.

This was too close.

They were very small pistols, but small ones tended to be highly inaccurate. She might hurt him by accident. But no, they couldn't be loaded. He wouldn't shoot her and he couldn't possibly want her to shoot him.

Could he?

This was absurd. He was doing it on purpose to aggravate her. Whimsical, indeed.

Mr. Bates said, "Miss Renfrew will ask if you are ready, then count to two, and give the word to fire. Is that clear?"

Lord Lovedon nodded.

Chloe nodded, though nothing was at all clear.

"Ready?" Amy called out.

No, I'm not even slightly ready.

"One."

Chloe sucked in air.

"Two."

She let it out.

"Fire."

Lord Lovedon raised his pistol and pointed it at her.

Trust me.

He fired.

A little blue and green bird sprang up from between the two barrels.

It twirled and fluttered its wings and sang, "Tweet tweet tweet tweet tweet."

*H*er face was a picture. Lovedon had all he could do to maintain his composure.

Then laughter spilled out of her, great gulps and whoops and funny little snorts.

"Your turn, Miss Sharp," he said.

She turned away, laughing, holding her pistol to her belly.

He stood watching her, marveling at the exuberance and joy of her. She laughed in the same way she'd defended her sister: with all her heart.

"Miss Sharp," he said.

She went off into whoops again. Then she wiped her eyes on the sleeve of her dress and returned to her dueling stance—body sideways, her glowing face straight on, pistol at her side. She brought up the pistol and fired.

A little blue and green bird popped up between the barrels and fluttered its wings and turned its head this way and that, so wondrously like a real bird, and it tweeted in the cheerful, beckoning way of a bird seeking its mate.

For a time, their birds tweeted and flirted with each other.

She watched the birds. When they stilled, she looked at him.

"I see," she said in a trembling voice. "They're French."

"I would say excessively so."

She held out the singing bird pistol. He took it from her, letting his hand graze hers. He put the birds back into their respective hiding places in the devices, then stepped away to return them to the pistol case, which Bates had left on the ground nearby. When Lovedon rose, he saw the two seconds walking back to the carriages, leaving the duelists to sort themselves out.

He turned to her.

She stood watching him. Her expression had grown serious, and he couldn't read it.

He grew anxious. If he muddled this part, he was finished.

"I realize I made a very bad first impression," he said. "But I can't apologize. If I hadn't behaved ill, you wouldn't have behaved ill, and then where should we be?"

"Not in Battersea Fields, certainly," she said. "This . . . it . . . ." Her lower lip trembled. Her eyes filled.

She covered her face and wept then, great, racking sobs, as uninhibited as her laughter.

Heart pounding, he closed the distance between them and wrapped his arms about her and held her.

The storm abated as suddenly as it had begun. After a moment, she tried to draw away. He didn't let go. "I only want to know I'm forgiven," he said.

"I forgive you," she said. "That was not what I . . ." She paused and swallowed. "My sister was going away, and I was so sure I couldn't be happy again, for a very long time."

"And now?"

She didn't answer, but she pushed, harder this time, and reluctantly he released her. She'd felt right in his arms. She'd felt right, he realized, from the moment she'd slapped him with her glove.

She started to turn away.

"You did the right thing," he said, "calling me to account."

She waved this away. "I was pot-valiant."

"You'd have done it even if you'd been fully sober," he said. "You might have done it differently, but you would have acted—out of love and loyalty and . . . all the right things."

She turned back to him, surprised.

"I want to make reparations," he said.

"You've done that," she said. Her expression

grew wry. "What a horrid waking up I had today."

"I've had my share of those," he said.

"You said you'd seen drunken friends home before," she said. "I've never done anything like that before in my life."

"Perhaps I bring out something special in you," he said.

"I was *mortified*," she said. "I was positive it would be years before I could look myself in the eye, let alone you." She looked up. "I begin to understand why men do it. A duel clears the air and settles everything."

"And one can be friends again," he said.

"We can't be friends again," she said. "We weren't friends *before*. Our worlds would never have overlapped if not for Althea's marrying Prince Louis."

"The world changes on that *if*," he said. "We met, we had words, we had a duel. And now that we've cleared the air, I should like to start over."

The color rising in her face told him she was beginning to understand what he was about.

"I beg that you won't judge me by my actions yesterday," he said.

She stared down at the toes of her purple boots. "They were not, all things considered, *consistently* bad actions," she said.

"I improve on acquaintance, people say," he

said. "Well, Bates wouldn't say it, but one must bear in mind that he's lately had a severe disappointment in love, which makes him bitter and quarrelsome. However, Miss Renfrew seems well able to hold her own with him, and really, I don't care much about them. I only care whether you will do me the honor of allowing me to take you for a drive in Hyde Park tomorrow afternoon."

She stared at her boots for quite a long time. She bit her lip.

He waited, calm on the outside, while his heart attempted to break all previous speed records.

Finally she looked up. "Are you quite sure?" she said.

Speeches wanted to tumble out of him, wild declarations. But that was mad. They'd met only yesterday. He would take this one step at a time, if it killed him.

"Quite," he said.

CASTLE DE GREY, FOUR WEEKS LATER

Lovedon drew Chloe into the passage between the drawing room and the picture gallery.

"It was here, wasn't it?" Lovedon said. "This was where you heard me talking rot about Prince Louis and your sister."

"Yes," she said. "But this isn't an immense royal wedding, only a dinner party, and we'll be missed."

"Let them miss us," he said.

He'd arranged the dinner party with his cousin the Duchess of Marchmont. She would have a very good idea why Lovedon had slipped out of the drawing room with Miss Sharp. Being far from conventional, Her Grace would cover up for them.

He wrapped his arms about Chloe and kissed her, firmly, so that there would be no question about it, and lingeringly, so that she wouldn't forget it in a hurry. And yes, certainly, he did it because he needed to and had needed to for what felt like eternity.

"There," he said, when he was sure he'd done the job properly. She started to pull away, but she stumbled, and he caught her about the waist. Her perfect waist, that went with the rest of her perfect body.

"I am not drunk," she said.

"I know that," he said. "I shouldn't have sneaked you in here if you were. You need to be completely in your senses."

"That's impossible, after what you just did," she said.

Her voice was a little husky, and even in the

passage's dim light, he saw the soft glow in her eyes.

"Somewhat in your senses will be sufficient," he said. "But not dead drunk. That wouldn't be fair. And I need you to answer more or less rationally." He went on in a rush, "I meant to take this in slow stages, but I'm so stupidly in love with you that slow and steady is only going to drive me mad."

"In love," she said softly.

"Yes, of course. How could I not be? I meant to be romantic, but this was the best I could do on short notice. That is, I didn't mean it to be short notice. I meant to wait until at least Tuesday next, but preferably until September. But there you were, sitting across the dinner table, and I was thinking how agreeable it would be if we could go upstairs to the same bedroom, instead of separate houses, and you could sit in my lap instead of all the way across the table on a chair. And then . . ." He trailed off because his brain was conjuring images that activated his breeding organs while deadening his powers of speech and clear thinking.

He sounded, in short, like a complete nitwit.

"I'm trying to decide," she said, "whether this is meant to be an offer of carte blanche or a proposal of marriage."

"I adore you," he said.

"That declaration could take things either way," she said.

"My dear Chloe, if you don't marry me, I'll do something rash."

"By which you mean, I presume, hitting yourself in the head repeatedly with the singing bird pistols until you lose consciousness and I take pity on you and say yes."

"I will certainly do that if necessary."

"Oh, you're the most ridiculous man. Of course I'll say yes. I was saying yes, very likely, at the same moment I threw champagne in your face. And I think it's the most romantic thing in the world, your proposing in this passage, instead of properly, on your knees in, say, our drawing room."

"I hoped you'd think that."

"You knew I'd think that," she said. "It's a tragic thing, but our minds are strangely alike."

"Yes, but I love you anyway," he said. He pulled her close again. "And I challenge you to put up with me until death us do part."

She reached up and caught him about the neck. "My lord," she said, "the satisfaction which your lordship has demanded, it is of course impossible for me to decline."

$\mathcal{D}$espite Lord Lovedon's impatience, the marriage had to wait for the bride's dress and the bridesmaids' dresses, and these things take time if they're to be done properly. Since every item issuing from Maison Noirot was always done properly, it was nearly September before Chloe Sharp became Lady Lovedon.

They were married, naturally, in the Gold Drawing Room of Castle de Grey, and the laughing way they looked at each other at the end—so obviously sharing a private joke—told all the world that yes, undoubtedly, they'd married for love.

Author's Note

*N*ot only are the singing bird pistols based on historical fact, but they still exist. To watch these wondrous mechanical devices in action, please go to:

http://www.christies.com/singing-bird-pistols-en-1422-3.aspx

And now a sneak peek at
New York Times bestselling author
Loretta Chase's

SILK IS FOR SEDUCTION

Available now

PROLOGUE

*I*n the summer of 1810, Mr. Edward Noirot eloped to Gretna Greene with Miss Catherine DeLucey.

Mr. Noirot had been led to believe he was eloping with an English heiress whose fortune, as a result of this rash act, would become his exclusively. An elopement cut out all the tiresome meddling, in the form of marriage settlements, by parents and lawyers. In running off with a blue-blooded English lady of fortune, Edward Noirot was carrying on an ancient family tradition: His mother and grandmother were English.

Unfortunately, he'd been misled by his intended, who was as accomplished in lying and cheating, in the most charming manner possible, as her lover was. There had indeed been a fortune. Past tense. It had belonged to her mother, whom

John DeLucey had seduced and taken to Scotland in the time-honored fashion of his own family.

The alleged fortune by this time was long gone. Miss DeLucey had intended to improve her financial circumstances in the way women of her family usually did, by luring into matrimony an unsuspecting blue-blooded gentleman with deep pockets and a lusting heart.

She, too, had been misled, because Edward Noirot had no more fortune than she did. He was, as he claimed, the offspring of a French count. But the family fortune had been swept away, along with the heads of various relatives, years before, during the Revolution.

Thanks to this comedy of errors, the most disreputable branch of one of France's noble families was united with its English counterpart, better known—and loathed—in the British Isles as the Dreadful DeLuceys.

The reader will easily imagine the couple's chagrin when the truth came out shortly after they'd made their vows.

The reader will undoubtedly expect the screaming, crying, and recriminations usual on such occasions. The reader, however, would be mistaken. Being the knaves they were—and furthermore quite truly in love—they laughed themselves sick. Then they joined forces. They set about seducing and swindling every dupe who crossed their path.

It was a long and convoluted path. It took them back and forth between England and the Continent, depending on when a location became too hot for comfort.

In the course of their wanderings, Catherine and Edward Noirot produced three daughters.

Chapter One

THE LADIES' DRESS-MAKER. Under this head we shall include not only the business of a Mantua Maker, but also of a Milliner . . . In the Milliner, taste and fancy are required; with a quickness in discerning, imitating, and improving upon various fashions, which are perpetually changing among the higher circles.

*The Book of English Trades,
and Library of the Useful Arts, 1818*

London
March 1835

Marcelline, Sophia, and Leonie Noirot, sisters and proprietresses of Maison Noirot, Fleet Street, West Chancery Lane, were all present when Lady Renfrew, wife of Sir Joseph Renfrew, dropped her bombshell.

Dark-haired Marcelline was shaping a papillon bow meant to entice her ladyship into purchasing Marcelline's latest creation. Fair-haired Sophia was restoring to order one of the drawers ransacked earlier for one of their more demanding customers. Leonie, the redhead, was adjusting the hem of the lady's intimate friend, Mrs. Sharp.

Though it was merely a piece of gossip dropped casually into the conversation, Mrs. Sharp shrieked—quite as though a bomb *had* gone off—and stumbled and stepped on Leonie's hand.

Leonie did not swear aloud, but Marcelline saw her lips form a word she doubted their patrons were accustomed to hearing.

Oblivious to any bodily injury done to insignificant dressmakers, Mrs. Sharp said, "The Duke of Clevedon is *returning*?"

"Yes," said Lady Renfrew, looking smug.

"To London?"

"Yes," said Lady Renfrew. "I have it on the very best authority."

"What happened? Did Lord Longmore threaten to shoot him?"

Any dressmaker aspiring to clothe ladies of the upper orders stayed au courant with the latter's doings. Consequently, Marcelline and her sisters were familiar with all the details of this story. They knew that Gervaise Angier, the seventh

Duke of Clevedon, had once been the ward of the Marquess of Warford, the Earl of Longmore's father. They knew that Longmore and Clevedon were the best of friends. They knew that Clevedon and Lady Clara Fairfax, the eldest of Longmore's three sisters, had been intended for each other since birth. Clevedon had doted on her since they were children. He'd never shown any inclination to court anyone else, though he'd certainly had liaisons aplenty of the other sort, especially during his three years on the Continent.

While the pair had never been officially engaged, that was regarded as a mere technicality. All the world had assumed the duke would marry her as soon as he returned with Longmore from their Grand Tour. All the world had been shocked when Longmore came back alone a year ago, and Clevedon continued his life of dissipation on the Continent.

Apparently, someone in the family had run out of patience, because Lord Longmore had traveled to Paris a fortnight ago. Rumor agreed he'd done so specifically to confront his friend about the long-delayed nuptials.

"I believe he threatened to horsewhip him, but of that one cannot be certain," said Lady Renfrew. "I was told only that Lord Longmore went to Paris, that he said or threatened something, with the result that his grace promised to return to London before the King's Birthday."

Though His Majesty had been born in August, his birthday was to be celebrated this year on the 28th of May.

Since none of the Noirot sisters did anything so obvious as shriek or stumble or even raise an eyebrow, no onlooker would have guessed they regarded this news as momentous.

They went on about their business, attending to the two ladies and the others who entered their establishment. That evening, they sent the seamstresses home at the usual hour and closed the shop. They went upstairs to their snug lodgings and ate their usual light supper. Marcelline told her six-year-old daughter, Lucie Cordelia, a story before putting her to bed at her usual bedtime.

Lucie was sleeping the sleep of the innocent—or as innocent as was possible for any child born into their ramshackle family—when the three sisters crept down the stairs to the workroom of their shop.

Everyday, a grubby little boy delivered the latest set of scandal sheets as soon as they were printed—usually before the ink was dry—to the shop's back door. Leonie collected today's lot and spread them out on the worktable. The sisters began to scan the columns.

"Here it is," Marcelline said after a moment. " 'Earl of L____ returned from Paris last night . . . We're informed that a certain duke, currently residing in the French capital, has been told in no uncertain terms that Lady C_____ was done awaiting his pleasure . . . his grace expected to return to London in time for the King's Birthday . . . engagement to be announced at a ball at Warford House at the end of the Season . . . wedding before summer's end.' "

She passed the report to Leonie, who read, " 'Should the gentleman fail to keep his appointment, the lady will consider their "understanding" a *misunderstanding.*' " She laughed. "Then follow some interesting surmises regarding which gentleman will be favored in his place."

She pushed the periodical toward Sophia, who was shaking her head. "She'd be a fool to give him up," she said. "A dukedom, for heaven's sake. How many are there? And an unmarried duke who's young, handsome, and healthy? I can count them on one finger." She stabbed her index finger at the column. "Him."

"I wonder what the hurry is about," Marcelline said. "She's only one and twenty."

"And what's she got to do but go to plays, operas, balls, dinners, routs, and so on?" said Leonie. "An aristocratic girl who's got looks, rank, and a respectable dowry wouldn't ever have to worry about attracting suitors. This girl . . ."

She didn't have to complete the sentence.

They'd seen Lady Clara Fairfax on several occasions. She was stunningly beautiful: fair-haired and blue-eyed in the classic English rose mode. Since her numerous endowments included high rank, impeccable lineage, and a splendid dowry, men threw themselves at her, right and left.

"Never again in her life will that girl wield so much power over men," Marcelline said. "I say she might wait until her late twenties to settle down."

"I reckon Lord Warford never expected the duke to stay away for so long," said Sophy.

"He always was under the marquess's thumb, they say," Leonie said. "Ever since his father drank himself to death. One can't blame his grace for bolting."

"I wonder if Lady Clara was growing restless," Sophy said. "No one seemed worried about Clevedon's absence, even when Longmore came home without him."

"Why worry?" said Marcelline. "To all intents and purposes, they're betrothed. Breaking with Lady Clara would mean breaking with the whole family."

"Maybe another beau appeared on the scene— one Lord Warford doesn't care for," said Leonie.

"More likely Lady Warford doesn't care for other beaux," said Sophy. "She wouldn't want to let a dukedom slip through her hands."

"I wonder what threat Longmore used," Sophy said. "They're both reputed to be wild and violent. He couldn't have threatened pistols at dawn. Killing the duke would be antithetical to his purpose. Maybe he simply offered to pummel his grace into oblivion."

"That I should like to see," Marcelline said.

"And I," said Sophy.

"And I," said Leonie.

"A pair of good-looking aristocratic men fighting," Marcelline said, grinning. Since Clevedon had left London several weeks before she and her sisters had arrived from Paris, they hadn't, to date, clapped eyes on him. They were aware, though, that all the world deemed him a handsome man. "There's a sight not to be missed. Too bad we shan't see it."

"On the other hand, a duke's wedding doesn't happen every day—and I'd begun to think this one wouldn't happen in our lifetime," Sophy said.

"It'll be the wedding of the year, if not the decade," Leonie said. "The bridal dress is only the beginning. She'll want a trousseau and a completely new wardrobe befitting her position. Everything will be of superior quality. Reams of blond lace. The finest silks. Muslin as light as air. She'll spend thousands upon thousands."

For a moment, the three sisters sat quietly contemplating this vision, in the way pious souls contemplated Paradise.

Marcelline knew Leonie was calculating those thousands down to the last farthing. Under the untamable mane of red hair was a hardheaded businesswoman. She had a fierce love of money and all the machinations involving it. She labored lovingly over her ledgers and accounts and such. Marcelline would rather clean privies than look at a column of figures.

But each sister had her strengths. Marcelline, the eldest, was the only one who physically resembled her father. For all she knew, she was the only one of them who truly was his daughter. She had certainly inherited his fashion sense, imagination, and skill in drawing. She'd inherited as well his passion for fine things, but thanks to the years spent in Paris learning the dressmaking trade from Cousin Emma, hers and her sisters' feelings in this regard went deeper. What had begun as drudgery—a trade learned in childhood, purely for survival—had become Marcelline's life and her love. She was not only Maison Noirot's designer but its soul.

Sophia, meanwhile, had a flair for drama, which she turned to profitable account. A fair-haired, blue-eyed innocent on the outside and a shark on the inside, Sophy could sell sand to Bedouins. She made stonyhearted moneylenders weep and stingy matrons buy the shop's most expensive creations.

"Only think of the prestige," Sophy said. "The Duchess of Clevedon will be a leader of fashion. Where she goes, everyone will follow."

"She'll be a leader of fashion in the right hands," Marcelline said. "At present . . ."

A chorus of sighs filled the pause.

"Her taste is unfortunate," said Leonie.

"Her mother," said Sophy.

"Her mother's dressmaker, to be precise," said Leonie.

"Hortense the Horrible," they said in grim unison.

Hortense Downes was the proprietress of Downes's, the single greatest obstacle to their planned domination of the London dressmaking trade.

At Maison Noirot, the hated rival's shop was known as *Dowdy's.*

"Stealing her from Dowdy's would be an act of charity, really," said Marcelline.

Silence followed while they dreamed their dreams.

Once they stole one customer, others would follow.

The women of the beau monde were sheep. That could work to one's advantage, if only one could get the sheep moving in the right direction. The trouble was, not nearly enough high-ranking women patronized Maison Noirot because none of their friends did. Very few were ready to try something new.

In the course of the shop's nearly three-year existence, they'd lured a number of ladies, like Lady Renfrew. But she was merely the wife of a recently knighted gentleman, and the others of their customers were, like her, gentry or newly rich. The highest echelons of the ton—the duchesses and marchionesses and countesses and such—still went to more established shops like Dowdy's.

Though their work was superior to anything their London rivals produced, Maison Noirot still lacked the prestige to draw the ladies at the top of the list of precedence.

"It took ten months to pry Lady Renfrew out of Dowdy's clutches," said Sophy.

They'd succeeded because her ladyship had overheard Dowdy's forewoman, Miss Oakes, say the eldest daughter's bodices were difficult to fit correctly, because her breasts were shockingly mismatched.

An indignant Lady Renfrew had canceled a huge order for mourning and come straight to

Maison Noirot, which her friend Lady Sharp had recommended.

During the fitting, Sophy had told the weeping eldest daughter that no woman in the world had perfectly matching breasts. She also told Miss Renfrew that her skin was like satin, and half the ladies of the beau monde would envy her décolleté. When the Noirot sisters were done dressing the young lady, she nearly swooned with happiness. It was reported that her handsomely displayed figure caused several young men to exhibit signs of swooning, too.

"We don't have ten months this time," Leonie said. "And we can't rely on that vicious cat at Dowdy's to insult Lady Warford. She's a marchioness, after all, not the lowly wife of a mere knight."

"We have to catch her quickly, or the chance is gone forever," said Sophy. "If Dowdy's get the Duchess of Clevedon's wedding dress, they'll get everything else."

"Not if I get there first," Marcelline said.

*G*ive in to your Impulses!

These unforgettable stories only take a second to buy and give you hours of reading pleasure!

Go to *www.AvonImpulse.com* and see what we have to offer.

Available wherever e-books are sold.

AVONIMPULSE

IMP 0811